CW00507814

T.M. Cooks is the pen name of the following collaborative writing team. The contributors are;

- Ridwaanah Alamin

- Kira Lim

- Harinie Suthakaran

- Mahnoor Ali Khan

- Schana Ghafury

- Hannah Conlon

- Cleo Gaynor

- Maria Qayyum

- Isabella Caris Smith

with cover design by Eleanna Fairhurst. The project was overseen by Joe Reddington.

The group cheerfully acknowledges the wonderful help given by:

- Eleanor Dixon

- Martin Mirshemirani

And a big thank you goes to Tolworth Girls' School who funded this wonderful project.

It's been a wonderful opportunity, and everyone involved has been filled with incredible knowledge and enthusiasm.

Finally, we would like to thank all staff at Tolworth Girls' School for their support in releasing our novelists from lessons for a full week.

The group started to plan out their novel at 8.30am on Monday 25th March 2019 and completed their last proofreading at 2pm on Friday 29th March 2019.

We are incredibly proud to state that every word of the story, every idea, every chapter and yes, every mistake, is entirely their own work. No teachers, parents or other students touched a single key during this process, and we would ask readers to keep this in mind.

We are sure you will agree that this is an incredible achievement. It has been a true delight and privilege to see this group of young people turn into professional novelists in front of our very eyes.

Paint Drying

T. M. Cooks

Contents

1

Parents: Dead. Sister: Dead. Memories: lost. All he has is a painting.

Unaccepted, confused and angry, Hero has lost his identity. He doesn't know who he is, where he is, or what happened. But something feels wrong. Stuck in hospital, Hero has flashbacks of people he doesn't recognise and when he paints the girl he keeps seeing, he realises that he may be closer to her then he thinks

With all these flashbacks, coming to life in his head,

Will he be able to find the truth?

Chapter 1

Goodbyes Are Never Easy

Sirens filled the air while the tow truck pulled a destroyed silver car out of the lake, disturbing the local wildlife. The surrounding mud had tyre tracks in it and the small wooden fence had been smashed through the middle. The road was blocked off but the pedestrians could still see the wreckage. Police looked around for witnesses but there where none. A few minutes later two ambulances drove through the broken fence and not long afterwards two bodies were wheeled into them. Later in the hospital, devastating news was delivered to the family.

When the family had found a parking space, the children ran out of the car and into the hospital building, their babysitter not far behind them. When they were inside, the twins were overwhelmed by bright lights and the sheer amount of people. The line for the reception desk took only a few minutes but to them it felt like an eternity. They grew restless; the children were desperate to see their parents. Finding the hospital room took a while though. The three of them were concerned and anxious, unaware of what was to come.

Room 91B, ground floor, second door to the left. They had found it, but were too late. The ECG had gone flat and the bodies where stone cold. The doctor took one look at the twelve-year-old kids sitting outside the room door and knew that this was not going to be easy. He stared at their pale faces then and with all his courage, he walked towards them.

"Excuse me, are you here for Mr and Mrs Thomas?" he inquired. Slowly they all nodded.

"Come with me please." he requested.

"NO!" Helly sobbed. The girl had clear crystal blue eyes but at that moment, they had a fire within them, almost like rage -

but mainly desperation. Salty tears were streaming down her face, she was struggling to breathe. Her world crumbled down around her. As hard as it was, Helly's heart had decided for her; she had accepted it, her twin, Hero didn't.

"When? Why did this happen?" The babysitter inquired.

"Earlier this evening. We don't know the full story yet but the grip on the wheel was lost and the car shot off the side of the road. I'm so sorry we couldn't do more." he sympathised.

Helly couldn't take it anymore. She fled the doctor's office and ran out into the corridor, out of the building and ran to the car. Unsure of what she was supposed to do once she got there, she sat on the floor, curled up into a ball and wept.

Meanwhile, Hero stayed silent. He was too stunned to react to what he was being told. Car crash found in a lake dead? It was all too much for him. He didn't believe it; he didn't want to believe it. Unaware of the tears that spilled from his eyes, he was still disturbed by the news. Something didn't feel right, he felt alone; his sister not in the room with him. After all, she was the only one who understood how he really felt.

After they left the doctor's office, the babysitter thought it was best if they ate something and told Hero to go wait by the door. Seeing as he lost his appetite, Hero went to search for his sister, scared that he's going to lose her too. Hero found her curled up in a ball by the car. He sat beside her and held her close, like he was going to lose her too. They both wept silently in that car park, holding each other tightly. Neither of them said anything at that point, nothing needed to be said.

A week of crying, heartbreak and misery goes by. Nobody sleeps, nobody smiles, nobody talks. At the end of the week the funeral comes along, no one could handle the agony that this day brought. A painful reminder to Hero and Helly that their parents are truly gone. At the funeral service, people gave speeches and there was a lot of crying especially from direct family and friends. Hero and Helly's Nana, cried the loudest. Losing a parent can be painful but losing a child can be much worse. Nana was upset despite most of her memories of her child being lost because of her dementia. That day, lots of people approached the twins with sympathy, they hated the fact that people tried to understand when they didn't. Hero nor Helly shed a tear when they were at the funeral, when they got back to Nana's place they cried themselves to sleep. Outside, the stars couldn't be seen and a darkness covered the town.

Meanwhile, their social worker was trying to find people who wanted to foster the twins. She couldn't imagine how hard this all was for them. *Who would want them? Who would treat them right?*

Chapter 2

A fresh start

The smell of food wafted through the house as Hannah waited for her husband to return home. Hannah felt herself being pulled into a warm embrace and looked up to see her husband's beautiful blue eyes and knew now was the time to tell him. Hannah spoke to her husband in a calm manner because she was afraid of his reaction.

"I went to the hospital today." Hannah whispered quietly.

"Why? Is something wrong?" his voice caring and worried.

"Well, the pregnancy test came negative." Hannah says crying.

"It's okay, right? We can try again, right?" he looked concerned.

"Well, the doctor said You s-see he told me-"

"He told you. What did he tell you." he interrupted her and grabbed her arms tight, which shook her.

"...I can't have children" her voice was low as can be and her husband's face slowly turned red.

"WHAT! You promised me when we got

married that I was going to have a son.
YOU TOLD ME!" Rachel starts to sob.
"Do you understand? I have been with
you through thick and thin and now you
tell me you can't and won't start an ac-
tual family with me I'm sorry but I can't
be with you if you can't have my child."
his voice bellows across the room.

"Please don't leave me if you go you
will miss out on the fun that we could
have together with our new foster children.
Think of the lives' we could change. Plus,
we would be able to have lots of different
children. If we adopt the child would not
be homeless and they would have a family
that love them."

"No I don't want that. I don't want
to be with you because you can't have my
child, we won't have the same experience

like the normal adults do and we won't have able to be a proper family, so it's time to say my goodbye, my love, I hope you have a good life with your children."

After Hannah's husband left her and she was left clueless because she didn't know that he would be that angry at her for thinking of fostering children. Hannah didn't think that she would ever be that lonely. She was thinking of fostering twins because then she would have some company, she needs someone in her life to feel happier. Hannah had finally stopped grieving she was sure she wanted to foster children.

A long time later, Hannah decided to go and talk to a social worker and tell them what she wanted to do. She didn't know how to tell her about it but she was sure that she wanted to foster. Driving to

Rachel's house Hannah became very nervous and she started to question herself "Am I able to be a foster mum?" "Will I be able to give them what they want?" "Will they like me?"

Hannah brought the car to an immediate halt and starts to sob, salty tears ran down her perfectly shaped head and fell into her lap. At this point she knew that her decision would affect everyone. Hannah pulled herself together and started up her rusty car. Driving slowly down the long narrow road, Hannah finally reached Rachel's house.

Rachel sees Hannah's car pulled up on her drive and she ran out the door and greeted Hannah.

"Hello Hannah" Rachel shouted with a massive warm smile on her face.

"Rachel!" Hannah replied with a hug.

"What brings you here at this time?" Said Rachel leading Hannah into her house.

"Well, I've been thinking a lot about becoming a foster mum and I think I'm ready to take on a foster child!" Hannah explained.

"Oh really, are you sure you are ready? You have been through a lot recently so remember you don't have to rush into anything." Rachel's said sounding concerned.

"No, no, I have been thinking about this for ages and I have finally come to a conclusion. I'm ready to foster my first child." Hannah said raising her voice slightly.

"I will do what I can but know that if you ever doubt it then inform me" Rachel replied.

Hannah is relieved that Rachel approves.

18

"Thank you so much Rachel, I hope I can get a child soon!"

Rachel looked in her diary and she gave Hannah a smile.

After a cup of tea and some lunch Rachel gets a phone call and leaves the room. A few minutes later Rachel returns with a humongous smile on her face, Hannah immediately knew that Rachel had heard good news. Rachel explains to Hannah that her boss told her that there are two teenage twins available for immediate fostering. Rachel tells Hannah that she thinks she is the right person to foster them. It took Rachel a lot of persuading to do but at the end she managed to convince her. Whilst Hannah had put a lot of thought into it she realised that she had tried to naturally make kids for so long but she could not have any so her fostering the twins would be a great opportunity for her. She felt terrible about not being able to naturally have kids but she knew that fostering kids might not mean that they would be related however she knew that they could try and make a family. Grinning with joy Hannah tells Rachel that she is ready to meet the twins. chapterA new parent

Hannah was looking forward to fostering her new children. She imagined how great life would be with two more people in the house but first she had to talk to the social worker in order to know how to take care of them and what responsibilities she would have once she fostered them. Hannah was very nervous to meet

the twins. As the social worker opened up
the door Hannah said "Give me a minute
to think this through." Slowly Hannah
takes a deep breath in, the social worker
replies "Take your time, it will be ok."
once Hannah is ready to go they enter and
the social worker introduced, Hannah to
the twins. Nervously, Hannah said "Hello,
my name is Hannah Gaylon, what are your
names" the twins just looked at her and
the boy replied "My name is Hero and this
is my sister Helly."

After meeting the twins Hannah felt a
huge wave of relief wash over her as the
seemed to really get along . Hannah and
Rachel started to fill the papers that Hannah had to fill in while Hero and Helly dis-
cuss Hannah.

"Do you like Hannah, she will be our

new foster mum." Hero asked Helly.

Helly replies back to her brother,

"I like Hannah, I hope she will be a good mother."

Hero replies back to his sister Helly,

"She will be good; I can see it will be the best for us"

Helly said back "Ok I trust you on this."

Once they both agreed on everything Hannah started to fill in the papers that took over forty-five minutes. She could not wait any longer she wanted to take the twins home and show them the house and their rooms.

Now when the papers were ready, Hannah was allowed to bring the them home. When the twins met Hannah they found her really kind and caring and they knew that she would be a great foster mum, they could not wait to see where they were staying. On the way home they were sitting in the car and there was an awkward moment of silence until the foster mum began to explain that she had a big house and that they would have so much fun together.

When they arrived at Hannah's house they were immediately showed to their rooms and they were given time to unpack.

Once Hero and Helly finished unpacking they started to make their way downstairs where Hannah had already prepared dinner. It was already on the table. She had made lasagne with some garlic bread on the side. They all sat down at the dinner table and began to eat. There was a long moment of silence and all you could hear was the cutlery hitting the plate.

Hero and Helly asked if they would meet

their dad which then made Hannah lose her appetite and feel uncomfortable. She felt a long shiver run down her spine. Seconds later she explained why they don't have a foster father. Hannah told them that she could not naturally have any children and once Hannah told her husband that she wanted to foster children he started to show hate towards her and he left. She did not feel comfortable talking about this but she knew she could trust Helly and Hero also they were family now which meant that she could not hide her feelings from them forever.

After dinner Hannah and the twins watched films and played board games. It felt like they were

meant to be together. At 9:30pm the twins went up to bed and Hannah laid on the sofa bed excitedly, thinking about the future they would all together.

Chapter 3

A cup of tea with a hint of sadness

It has been eight years and Helly and Hero have grown used to life with Hannah. They have accepted her as their mother. However, they never forget to visit there nana. Usually, Helly and Hero visit together but today Helly decided to visit alone.

"So my love, how has your week been?" Nana said in a soft voice.

"I've been really busy doing all my work." Helly replies.

The sound of the whistling kettle filled the room, where Nana and Helly sat. Nana is telling Helly about her long and hard life. Helly began to ask Nana questions about Nana's dad being in the war, and Nana happily told Helly what she could remember of her life story.

"How is school?" Nana asked "Do you have a boyfriend?"

Helly started to act nervous and strange. After a lot of thinking Helly pulls herself together and decides to tell her Nana what was going on inside her head. Helly thought of ways to tell her Nana how she felt without upsetting her. She didn't know what to say to Nana so she stayed quiet for a minute until her Nana said something. Helly started to play with her hands and hung her head in sadness. Helly decided that she was not going to wait any longer and she asked her Nana if she could tell her something that is really important. Nana told Helly that she could always talk to her about anything she's worried about and that Nana will always listen to her. Helly told Nana all the things that are going on in her life and Nana advised her with what to do.

They both had a conversation about all of Helly's issues Nana helped Helly sort out some things that were on her mind. Helly told Nana more things that she wanted help with and Nana suggested ways of coping with the situation. Helly began to become more confident with telling Nana about her issues and liked the advice that Nana was gave her. Finally, when Helly finished telling Nana about her issues she felt a lot happier about her life. Helly started to agree with what Nana was said. Nana carried on giving Helly advice about her queries and Helly started to agree with what Nana was telling her. Nana is concerned about Helly's abusive boyfriend and didn't know what to do about the situation. Helly told Nana how he hits her when she doesn't do something right and how he would pull her hair when she says something wrong. Nana asked Helly if James ever treats her right and Helly hung her head in shame. Helly didn't want to tell Nana how James treats her all the time but

she wanted Nana to give her advice. Nana
tells Helly that she needed to get professional help and that she needed to speak
with a therapist. Helly tells Nana that she
didn't want to make a fuss about it and
she just wanted to get on with her life and
forget about it all.

Nana told her ways of getting out of
the relationship and told Helly that she
would help Nana explained to Helly that
she needed to get out of the relationship
with James and sort her life out. Helly
replied to Nana and said that she still loves
James even though he abuses her but she
just can't stay with him anymore. Helly
explained to Nana that she was tired of
James treating her like rubbish and abus-
ing her just because he has a bad day.
Nana understood where Helly was coming

from and agreed to help Helly end the relationship between her and James. Nana and Helly discussed a plan on how to end the relationship between them. They both decided that it would be best for Helly to tell James how she feels about their relationship and see what he says about it. Helly began to act very strange. Nana became worried about the bad decisions that Helly might make. Nana explained to Helly that she should think deeply about her decisions before she made them because Helly could end up in danger.

Helly's trembling hand reached towards her cup as she thought about how to end this relationship. *Was she ready to stand up against James? Or was she thinking of something else? Something worse*

Chapter 4

A shadow to never forget...

Helly reminisced about her time with James and how he looked every time he was alone. His eyes seemed distant and his face cold and shut away from the world; when she saw him like this it reminded her

33

of herself and Hero when they lost their parents. Eight years ago James' mum was ill, her face as white as the clouds. Sarah new that her time was almost up. The cancer had got to her brain right now and was making her heart go faster. The chemotherapy was no use; the doctor lied to James. His mum was not going to be okay. Sarah brought James closer and had kissed him on the forehead and told him that everything was going to be okay. Although, he was young he was old enough to know when his mum was lying to make him feel better. Her heart beat slowed down and she stopped moving. James could feel her hand grip weaken. There was a red button attached onto the back of the wall and he knew that once he pressed it they would come rushing in and he would never be able to have this time again. He never pressed the button.

One hour had passed before Dan had wanted to see his wife. Only one person was allowed to visited at a time. However, to him it didn't matter, his wife was in a critical state. He walked in. "Sarah? Sarah!". There was no response. The only thing that looked up was his sons little face, holding onto his mother's hand as if she was playing a game and at any moment she would wake up and be okay. "What do you think you are doing?" He pushed past his son and pressed the button. As quick as light, the nurses came in, but by the time they were their it was too late. Sarah, his mum was dead.

Dan didn't want a funeral for his wife. He said that she didn't want it that she just wanted to have her ashes spread out on a field. Just like her mothers. By the time they got home it was dark and raining. Dan went upstairs to his room and sat on his bed. James loved school, because of his mother telling him that in the future he can be anything he wanted to be as long as he believed and went to school.

"Why didn't you get someone? She could have been saved you ugly meniace!" Next morning was silent, only the sound of cutlery echoed in the silence and his father's glare. He held his sons' wrist and his grip got tighter. "It was too late; she was already...dead." James voice cowered into a whisper. He pulled his hands away from his dad and ran up the stairs. Before reaching the top he said" it's not my fault that mum died". However, that wasn't the end of it. Every day he would blame him for not telling a nurse or telling him or getting anyone. However, one day it escalated from it being at home to it being at school.

It was a monday morning the first time in four weeks that James had gone to school. He had missed a lot. He was alone the whole day; he couldn't tell if it was just because his mum had died so he was acting different or because his dad was screaming at him every day. By the time he came home from school his dad was drinking and had forgot to pick him up from school. James walked in. the TV was on however there was no signal so it was just black and white. The lights weren't turned on and Dan was just sitting on the sofa with a cup full of beer in his hand. "Sarah? Are you home", he turned around and came closer

to James. "you...you killed my wife." Dan
was ten times taller than James.

"Why did you have to kill her she was
so innocent?". He fair skin; her plump red
lips and her golden hair. He shoved James
into the wall and slapped him. "It's your
fault that my wife is dead. You don't de-
serve to be alive. Do you hear me?" his
eyes were burning scarlett and he threw
his glass on the ground. "Why Didn't you
get someone she could have been saved" he
held his son's wrist and his grip go tighter.
"You're such a stupid boy, it should have
been you with the cancer. You could have
experienced what it felt like to have cancer. What it felt like for you to need help.
For you need your own flesh and blood to
save your life!". That night was a night
that James will remember for the rest of

his life.

For the next eight years the same thing happens again and again. James bruises got bigger and he ate less and less. He was the same height and his father and would have had a good chance at taking him on, however no matter how big or strong he was he wasn't brave enough to face his dad face to face." What are you looking at?" His dad was weaker than before, and was living on benefits, because he lost his job after his dad died. "I'm going to work. Now move out my way." James face looked strong.

"No- matter how tough you look you will still be the same scared cat that you were five years ago."

He finished his drink "Get in the car, I can take you to work." James looked his dad in the face and thought if it would be the safest to go in a car with a drunk man. "No it's okay I'll walk to work". He stepped outside the door. A few minutes later before he had reached work, he got a phone call from the hospital. "H-Hello" The phone goes quiet for a few seconds before a response "We are really sorry to inform you that your father is in hospital, he has had a car accident and was not wearing a seatbelt. He has five different head injuries and wants to see..." James put the phone down and goes to the hospital. James stares at his dad for ten minutes in silence before a conversation starts. "I'm sorry dad I should have been there with you in that car. M-maybe if i was there I could have stopped this from happening." All his father does is look at him straight in the eye. "Please say something, I can't lose you too" Dan takes off the mask and slowly speaks making sure that every last breath counts "Don't worry son. I'm the one that should be saying sorry." James face lights up "I never knew what a disappointment you were. You are the last one in the family and you will die alone with no-one left to hold your hand. I have taken care of you for as long as you can remember and this is how you treat me. First you kill your mother, and then you kill me. I hate you, you are the worst son any father could have asked for. This is all your fault and you know it."

James took the pillow from the bed so his father lay uncomfortably his father looked confused. James eyes pierced through his father's, like a lion hunting his prey, silence flooded the room . "Dad? Dad...I'm sorry I didn't mean to, you made me so mad saying that I was a disappointment." He ran over to press the button, "Don't worry dad I'm not losing you too".it was already too late. His father was dead.

Chapter 5

The Approaching Death

Three years ago

A chill ran down her spine as she replaced her cozy, sweatshirt and flannel pajama pants with only a thin, blue hospital gown. She felt the bitter air against her bare back. She scurried as fast as she could to the gurney, escaping from the coldness of the tile floor that seeped through the paper slippers that she wore. No matter how she lay, she felt the need to continue tossing and turning, trying to find a comfortable position. This was especially difficult, considering the fact that this bed on wheels was only half the width of her twin sized bed at home but this bed shaked with even the slightest movement Kenya made. Finally, she gave up her quest to become comfortable and decided to look for something that kept her mind off of the edginess that she was feeling. The ceiling was composed of white, holey, rectangles with random stains of a faded brown. She began counting the rectangles from the front of the room to the back. Seven. Then she counted them from the very left of the room to the right. Nine. "The ceiling has sixty-three squares on it, " she pondered. Somehow this fascinated her so much that she was able to temporarily forget about her nervousness. "Hey, Dad, " She exclaimed. He looked up from behind the paperwork he was filling out for the doctor. "What's up, Kenya." He asked. Just as she was about to tell him her exhilarating news about the rectangles on the ceiling, she realized how ridiculous it was. Embarrassed at how pathetic her burst of excitement was, her face felt hot. She knew her cheeks were turning red so she turned her head away from her dad and casually asked, "What time is it?" His long, dark, eyes glanced down at his watch and he softly responded, "1:45pm." Only 1:45pm she thought to herself, "Is mum going to get Annie?" The little girl asked her dad. He nodded and he went back to the paperwork he was filling.

She spirits, breathlessly, towards a black shiny car. Her smile was as bright as a diamond, her caramel brown hair floated rapidly behind her shoulders, her black skirt flying up and down on her knees, as if to make a decision to stay or to be free, her sky blue eyes fixed on the figure in the car. She slowed down once she arrived at the side of the car, leaning in, she opened her mouth,

"Hey!" Her calm, gleeful voice spoke. The woman inside the car spoke softly, but hurriedly to her child,

"Hi, darling. Get hurrying now, Kenya has been waiting patiently throughout the day; you know how she can be."

The girl in the black blazer took long strides towards the side door of the car. She violently took off her bag and throws it on the other side of the red leather seats. The girl sat herself down in the middle seat,

"How was your day, love."

"Who me?"

"Yes, you."

"Oh you know the usual, boring." The caramel haired girl mumbled under her breath, obviously agitated. The mother looked in the mirror view a kind, encouraging smile was on her face, as she stared straight at the school girl,

"Sorry, Annie what was that, I didn't quite hear you."

Annie, rolling her eyes, replied, "Nothing, Maria."

"Excuse me young lady, what have I told you about calling your elders by their names?"

"Sorry, mother." The rest of the journey was awkward and dead quiet, neither of them dared to talk as if they were afraid to do so.

"STOP, STOP!" Annie roared at her mum. The car screeched and eventually comes to a stop.

"What?" Maria enquiried.

"I just didn't want to waste time walking from the car park to the reception so I wanted you to stop." Annie replied with a cheeky grin. She grabbed her bag and made her way outside without bothering to wait for her mother's reply. Rolling her eyes Maria laughed,

"Off you go then, remember the room number is thirteen and not thirty." With a laugh the girl carefully crossed the road and slowly walked towards the hospital building.

Annie looked behind her and shouted,

"That was yesterday and besides I'm feeling more mature today."

She sprinted towards the entrance. Gasping for air the young girl arrived at her destination. "Annie! Lovely to see you again. Would you like to take the lift?" The receptionist asked sweetly.

"Gretta, Hey! That would be great, I'm not sure if you could tell or not but I am exhausted."

Gretta chuckles and she opened the drawer then hands Annie the keys for the lift. Annie snatched it out of her hands and without a single glance back, she ran towards the lift.

"Your welcome, love." Gretta yelled after her, her voice still sweet as sugar.

The door finally slid open as the girl sped out of the lift towards room three, second floor in the Hospital of Hope. All that was left of her was the beautiful scent of her perfume that invaded the lift, the scent could make anyone come back to life. All it took for the little girl to get inside the room was one soft knock of desperation when a tall man with caramel hair, emerald eyes opened the door.

"Hi, Annie. How was school?" He whispered as if he was afraid to wake someone up. The man moved away from the door to let the little girl in. Annie took one big step inside the room.

"Dad, school was absolutely dull. I had no fun whatsoever." Annie whispered back. She slowly approaches the white bed sheet bed. On the bed laid a beautiful young girl, sleeping peacefully. Her face lifeless her once red lips blue. The little girl sat beside her father waiting for her mother to come. The door slowly opened leaving a creak' sound that echoed in the corridors.

"Hey, how is she, David?"

Maria made her way towards them placing herself beside Annie.

David spoke quietly, "She was in a mood when you left, the doctors and nurses found it impossible to calm her."

Maria's gaze moved onto her lovely daughter, she looked at her with sorrowful eyes, that filled up with tears.

It had been a long day and it was not

over yet. Annie sat there with her parents, waiting for it to be over. The waiting was the worst part. She didn't know if today was the last time she came here or if she will be back every day for the next nine months. She did not like hospitals. she didn't like the pain it brang people, people like her littler sister, Kenya. Annie didn't like the fear of not knowing whether someone was ever going to make it out of there or if this was how they will end their lives. It's lonely in the waiting room, like a Monday morning of school. Annie has had been coming here for a while now, visiting her sister. Hospitals scared Annie, she felt like she was the only one there. It was dark, the bright lights did nothing but blind her. She felt like a deer caught in the headlights. Nowhere to go and nowhere to hide. It's bitter and she could never seem to get warm. She wore extra clothes to try to keep the warmth in, but it didn't work. She could only sit there for so long without becoming nauseous. The stench, reminiscent of ammonia and bleach, only brang unpleasant memories. Annie needed air or she thought she might pass out. She could taste it, pungent. It was in the back of her throat, choking her. It was hushed, as if no one else was there.She only heard footsteps and they seemed so far away. Everyone was whispering for fear of speaking to loud will cause death. Maybe if they didn't talk about the inevitable, it will never come. The secrets, hiding from death when death is the one thing they can be sure is coming. The awful music; like a dentist's office, but worse. Occasionally it cuts out, when the reception comes over the microphone to page a doctor. She jump. Annie was anxious, she can't sit still; yet she can't get up to move. The looks on the faces of the people coming in and out, knowing how they are scared and confused. The emptiness in the eyes of those waiting for the doctors to come back with news. Not knowing if they will be leaving the hospital with the ones they love, or not.

Lost in a world of darkness, Kenya heard faint eerie whispers. She felt little like a small child lost in a dark cave, cold and all alone. Was she lost in some unfamiliar land; were those whispers coming from her loved ones in the far off distance? As time passed she became more coherent; voices became louder and were spoken with more clarity. Kenya felt something strange; it was lodged in her mouth and felt as if it was protruding deep into her throat. The feeling made Kenya feel very uncomfortable, the gagging feeling. She wanted to remove it more than anything. Kenya tried to tear it from her throat but her arms were restrained to her sides. She fought at her restraints with all her possible might; much like a prisoner in shackles trying to escape from the inevitable fate ensuing the reading of his final rites. With no avail she kept fighting but all her efforts were fruitless considering her weak condition. She probably never would have beaten her goal at a full capacity. Kenya heard then a voice, a voice of ascension. It was clear and inundating; it was almost omnipotent. She heard this voice of guidance telling her not to fight and that she is on a ventilator; he understood her discomfort and assured her that it was ok. She still kept fighting. Again the voice rang out in a more commanding tone,

"Kenya stay with us. KENYA!" She began to slowly fade out of her subtle reality. She didn't wake for some time later in a room surrounded by instruments that were connected to her chest and head. Kenya had a needle leaving her arm trailing back to several intravenous bags hanging over the bed she was laying in. These sights were all too familiar; she was in a hospital lying in the critical care unit. Then she recalled her temporary state of semi consciousness and recall hearing the voice, who she now assumed was the doctor, tell her she was going to live. The most pessimistic of thoughts came into her head. She looked around the room knowing this was her final day. Slowly she closed her eyes, she never opened them ever again.

Chapter 6

One Last Pain

Five Days After Kenya's Death

The sun shone brilliantly and the virulent colour of the spring day under its glare was

offensively bright and cheerful. It was as if they conspired to show Annie, David, and Maria how the world would go on without Kenya. It shouldn't. Everything should be as grey and foggy as their emotions, it should be cold and damp with silent air. But the birds still sang and the flowers still bloomed. They walked through the churchyard like a silhouette of themselves, wishing they were as insubstantial as the shadows so that their insides might not feel so mangled. Right now they were at a funeral. Their daughter's and sister's funeral The magnitude of desire in their eyes. As they took a pew near the front long held back tears began to flow. They loved her. Now she was gone a light had been extinguished forever in their hearts. The funeral was all black

and white clothes, every one of them with puffed red eyes.

Three Months later

They wait, the starlight and the silvery moon, the shadow of the trees upon the cedar fence. The leaves flickering like candlelight, creating a new picture from moment to moment. Amid the perfume blooms, feeling the cool of the evening. The waves kissed the sun-warm sand. The home phone rang for a thousandth time yet no one picked up. A pale, tall girl with sky blue eyes and redness underneath them, walks towards the ringing phone her straight caramel hair tied in a neat bun which followed behind her. She reaches for the phone.

"Hello?" Her voice barely a whisper.

"Hello?" A deep voice replied on the other side of the phone.

"Yes hi, who is this?"

"I'm Joshua from The Kemlet hospital a man named " But Annie didn't need a name to realise that something bad happened to her father. Tears strolls down her face.

"What's the name on the driving licence, Hina? ... David? David, did you know him?"

"Y..y.." The girl didn't have the time to even say yes' her eyes suddenly went foggy she slit out a horrible sob and knew if she continued she would never stop crying.

"Hello? Anyone there?"

"Mum! MUM! She screamed. A tall, pale, sky blue eyed woman came down the stairs her brown hair tied into a ponytail.

"What is it, Annie?"

"It's dad" Annie replied. The women spirits towards the phone. She snatches the phone from Annie, desperate to know what is going on. Voice shaking Maria talks on the phone,

"Hello..?"

The clouds, the colour of gloom, the golden leaves from the trees falls as slow as a snail. Nothing worse could have happened on that day, after all everything happens for a reason. On the 10th of April 2004 David Dexter died in a car accident. His funeral took place the next day at 4 pm sharp. Luckily his grave was right next to his daughter Kenya, a 12-year-old girl who had a dream of becoming a doctor, who suffered from cancer and unfortunately wasn't one of the

lucky survivors.

Chapter 7

More Drugs, less money

The sound of a discomforting sound woke, the twenty-year-old women, Annie. Rubbing her eyes, she made her way towards the unpleasant sound of glass scattering on the floor. Her eyes flew open, the sleep no longer haunting her, when she realises that her mum is responsible for the noises at midnight. "Mum! Mum! Mum what on Earth!!" Annie rapidly grabbed her mum before she could step on the sharp broken glass. "Oh hello, love. How are you?" Maria's shiny sky blue eyes told the truth, the truth that she had no idea what she was doing, the truth that she didn't want to be doing this, the truth that she felt helpless. The two of them where in the living room. A large TV at the far left side, on top of the heater, two large white fabric sofas opposite each other close to the TV and a small coffee table in the middle. Annie gently places her mum on the sofa white, cream fabric and spirits to on the light. Slowly the darkness left the room once more. Annie places herself down next to her mother. None of them spoke for what felt like eternity.

Maria stood up carefully trying not to wake up Annie who slept an hour before. She carefully went to the opposite side of the sofa and grabbed the heart shaped cushion, she unzipped the cushion and threw them on the floor. After twenty minutes the whole living room was a huge mess. All the sufferings of the cushion had been exploded around the room as if a cat had been in the room, the left hand side sofa has been dropped to the floor. Annie woke up at the noise of a large crash in the kitchen. Annie ran down to the kitchen. "Annie's voice outraged was echoing from miles away. Her mum shivered her heart pumped as fast as a racing car, still unaware of her surroundings and what she had done. Annie grabbed Maria's arm gently and pulled her upstairs, stopping each time to look at the blood streamed blood resending itself as a river. The room was incredibly large. The couch was cream but inlaid with a fine red silk: leaves embroidered so delicately that they might have landed there in spring, but Maria knew that they took hundreds of hours to sew. The white curtains were linen, the kind of white that was untouched by hands and devoid of dust. Carefully Annie set her mum on the bed. Then she jogged down to get a cloth to stop the bleeding of the foot, she saw her mum doing the same thing in the past when she fell down from her bike.

Maria couldn't handle the dreadful pain it was like waking up from a nightmare. "Clam down, mum. It's going to be alright." But as Annie said those very words she knew nothing was going to be okay everything was going the wrong, it just felt like a bitter lie she had been told her whole life but now it's her turn to continue. One foot behind the other, Annie walked towards her mother's purse as she wanted to buy sleeping pills to finally end the pain she was suffering from. As she had opened the zip her shaking hands slid inside the opened purse, mouth horrified she turned around to look at her terrified mother who was peacefully sleeping.

Closing the door of her mother's room Annie soundlessly went to her room. Her head spinning all over the place she thought about how she could help her mum, how she could pay for the medicines her mother desperately needed to take. Annie needed the money. Sitting on her bed she typed into her laptop. Several hours passed, Annie looked furious, annoyed that she could not find anything. After what felt like eternity Annie finally found the job she could be interested in. Ever since Annie's sister, Kenya, died Annie wanted to work at a place that helped young children, something that could advice young people to make reasonable decisions. Just like her sister once taught her. The sleep haunted her once more this time Annie had no chance of killing the tiredness. As rapidly as she could manage she filled the application form for becoming a therapist. Several hours had passed until an email from The Letra Surgery was received to Annie, accepting her request.

Annie could not stop worrying about

her new job she did not want to lose this one as well. She needed the money. She unlocked the door and slowly opened it letting herself in. Once Annie settled down in her room she remembered that she had a box filled with little fragile decorations she carefully placed them on her desk thinking of where she was going to put it. She already had some ideas but she wanted to wait until she knew where she wanted to put all of them.once she was ready she carefully hanged them up around the room.When her room felt welcoming enough she looked at her bookings and there was only one person who wanted to see her, which was Hero. Annie felt quite disappointed but it did not make her lose hope. Once Hero's appointment occurred she had no problem speaking to him because she had practised talking like a therapist before their appointment. The fact that she was new did not bother her, neither did the fact that she only has one appointment because she thought that the least she could do was help make someone's life better.

Chapter 8

Till death do us apart

"I can't take this anymore." Helly shouted enraged.

"Your supposed to be in a relationship to be happy, to smile, to laugh and make good memories not to constantly be scared, to feel hurt, to cry. You inflict pain on me in the most brutal ways possible, you lie and break promises yet every time you hurt me I apologize and feel guilty for making you feel bad." Water exploded out of Helly's eyes as she angrily carried on her rant.

"You hurt me so much that sometimes it feels like my heart is being ripped out of my chest and yet I'm dumb enough to stay, thinking I can fix you, that one day you will magically change but now I'm starting to realise that, that day is never gonna come" She shouts in hysterics

"I can't take anymore of this...of this abuse and the truth is you never deserved me" She screamed at the top of her lungs finding it hard to breath, hoping he would listen.

"I loved you and you knew but you broke me anyway. Why? What did I do to you?" She cried.

"You made me lose my friends, my family I have done everything you asked of me what more do you want?" screamed Helly.

James however, did not look pleased as he towered over Helly with a raised hand "Why can't you just shut up and do the world a favour, by dying instead of complaining all the time about your pathetic excuse of a life!" expressed James in rage.

"Why would I have to complain when I have such a fabulous boyfriend who controls every single thing I do, who cheats on me, almost every night and most importantly hits, slaps and kicks me" Helly sobs, "Your a psychopath who can't feel love and doesn't know what a real relationship is. You don't love me, the only reason you want this relationship is because you like the way I made you feel, for pleasure."

"You know what? Life would definitely be better off without me. When I die don't bother showing up to my grave I have had enough of you. I already know that you'll realise your mistakes when I'm gone, and a top tip is that with that attitude you will never get a girlfriend or even anywhere in life." Helly realised that she needed to calm down but the words just erupted out of her.

"You might want to stop depending on me, you need to learn how to work independently. Don't think I'm lying when I say that I won't be here one day and that's not even the worst part, the worst part is that you know how hard life has been for me but I still trusted you, you knew about my parents but you still decided to treat me like an animal not even an animal nothing is treated like this."

A couple of weeks later Helly did what she said. She committed suicide. On that day Rachel came to get the paperwork that were meant to be filled in but first she asked to go to the toilet. So when she got halfway there she saw a body lying on the floor in the toilet so she went to the toilet and went to see what happened. Rachel found Helly laying on the floor in the toilet with some tablets in her hand. Rachel tried her best to wake her up, since she looked like she was sleeping but it was no use so she called Hannah and said that they would take her to the hospital as soon as possible. It was not hard to believe that she would have done something like this since she has had so much going on in her life.

Rachel and Hannah still had hope of Helly living but when they arrived at the hospital Hannah began to cry, "I tried my best looking after her, she was like a daughter of my own." She mentioned.

You could feel sadness in the air. Just looking at Helly laying on the floor brought tears to Rachel's eyes. All Hannah thought about know was how she was going to tell Hero that Helly is in the hospital. Hannah knew that Hero would freak out so she thought that she should tell Hero before it was too late.

Hannah could not wait any longer, she called Hero and she slowly explained to him that Helly was at the hospital and that she had taken overdoses. Hero freaked out before Hannah could even finish her sentence. Hero rushed to the hospital and left everything that he was doing.

It did not take long until he got there but it was few seconds late. He looked enraged. Rachel was standing at the hospital door waiting for Hero to show him the way to her room.Hero His name was spinning through Rachel's mind. She was in front of the door, standing, waiting, hoping this feeling would disappear so she could focus on Hero. Hero, Hero, Hero. A twenty-year-old boy who just lost his twin sister. Rachel asked in her worried voice "Are you okay?"

"We are coping". Hannah sniffed as a tear fell down her face.

The doctor did explain that nobody was

allowed to go and see her since she needed to rest because she may not survive. But did Hero care? No, he rushed into the room trying to catch his breath but it was too late, his sister died the second he came into the room.

Weeks passed by and they still had not finished getting everything ready for the funeral however they could not wait any longer. Hero did not want to say goodbye he did not even want to think about losing Helly. Hero was furious he had lost his parents, he lost his sister and he did not see how anything in his life could get any worse. His life felt like a huge problem.

Chapter 9

A special goodbye

Nana's old care home had to be refurbished so Nana wouldn't be able to stay there for another five months and there is nowhere else for her to go, so she booked herself into a new care home. Nana has a bigger room and more storage. In this care home there were so many more things to do during the day such as board games, swimming and gardening. There are also so many more people in this care home for Nana to make friends with. Everybody is really welcoming.

Nana goes to her room and starts to unpack her stuff. She places all her clothes into her wardrobe and her drawers. Nana hangs up some pictures on her wall of her grandchildren and makes sure her room is all tidy. She then opens up her window and stares outside for a while after that she takes in a deep breath of fresh air and sighs to herself. Nana decides to have a rest.

Nana gets back from a day in the garden with her friends and starts to sort her possessions out in her drawers. She finds all sorts of pictures and drawings that she never knew existed. Nana looked deeper into the back of her draw and finds a letter in a brown envelope addressed to Hero from Helly. Nana wants to know what the letter says but she is too worried to open it.

Nana starts to get very worried about why Helly would leave a letter addressed to Hero and no one else. She began to rethink all the bad situations Helly had put herself in and tried to work out why.

Feeling puzzled Nana was left clueless on what to do with the letter. Thoughts rushed through her mind until she thought of a few ways to give the letter to Hero. Nana placed the letter on the window seal and got into bed.

The next morning the sun shone brightly down onto the bed of flowers, where Nana was gardening. Hero creeps up behind her and grabs her shoulders and shouts "Hi Nana"

"Oh my goodness... hello my boy, how are you." Nana replies with a jump.

"I'm good, how are you settling in?" Hero asks

"Very well, thank you, I am making new friends each day." Nana states.

Nana takes Hero up to her room and she shows him around.

Hero ask her some question and they both have a long conversation. When they reach Nana's room Nana forgets her gloves in the garden so she tells Hero to go inside while she goes to get them. Hero enters Nana's room and starts to look around. He glances at all the pictures on the walls, admiring all the ones of him and Helly. Hero goes over to the window to see if he can see Nana in the garden and notices something on the window seal. He picks up the brown envelope and turns it over, it is addressed to him.

Feeling confused Hero opens up the letter and begins to read

Dear Hero,

If you are reading this, then I'm so sorry for everything that I have put you through but you need to hear me out. I did this for a reason...

I am writing this to you to let you know that just because you can't see me does not mean that I am not with you. I will always be by your side even if you might not want me there. I believe in you and you don't always need me there, I know that we told each other everything but that does not have to change because I am right next to you even if you do not see me. You don't have to hide your feelings, be confident, be proud of who you are, stop being afraid of the world. I know that reading this may be hard for you but you can make it till the end, you always do. I did this because I felt that it was all too much for me, mum and dad dying, then the stress of school, but most importantly I wanted to tell you that my ex-boyfriend, James, abused me, I met him one day when I went out with my friends and he seemed really nice so we started talking for a while. Then he asked me out and I said yes because I thought he'd treat me right but it was a big mistake. After he started to hit me he raped me. He forced me not to tell anyone I tried to stand up to myself, but it was no use. I was stupid enough to think that he might change, but I was wrong. I wanted to tell you but I couldn't bring myself around to. I knew you would get angry with me. You were always there for me and I love you. You don't understand how thankful I am to have such an amazing twin brother like you.

I love you loads bro

Helly xxx

Tears drop from Hero's eyes and splash onto the letter. Nana slowly opens the door and see's Hero standing looking out the window.

"So you like my room?" Nana questions "Hero? Are you okay?"

She walks over to Hero to see his eyes

full of tears, "Oh my goodness Hero, what happened?"

"I read it." He replies softly

"Read what Hero? tell me." She asked worriedly

"I read the letter Nana." sobbed Hero

"Letter? Letter? ...Oh you found the letter." she repeats frantically "I'm so sorry, I was going to give it to you but I completely forgot."

"Don't worry about it, Nana I'll come and visit you during the week." Hero promised

"Oh you're going so soon, never mind don't forget I love you." She replied softly trying to hide her disappointment.

Chapter 10

Considering

After a long and tiring day, out with the care home Nana finally arrives back and goes straight to her room. She jumps straight into her bed and relaxes for the rest of the night.

Nana was just a few hours into a film when she was interrupted by her room phone ringing. She answered the phone and it was reception. They told Nana she had to go straight down to the front entrance and they would explain to her when she went down there. Nana grabbed her bag, put on her slippers and made her way downstairs. When Nana got down the stairs she was greeted in the reception area by Hero and the new foster mum, Hannah. Hannah looked at Nana and gave her a small smile, Nana gave Hannah a warm smile back. Nana went over to greet Hannah properly and Hannah took one long look into Nana's blue eyes and burst into tears.

Nana was left confused on why Hannah was standing in front of her crying until Hannah started to explain why she was there. Hannah told Nana that something had happened to Helly and it was very serious. Nana immediately knew that Helly had done something to herself. Hannah explained to Nana that Helly had unfortunately ended her life. Nana started to tear up as she fell to her knees as the salty tears slowly ran down her wrinkly face. Nana pulls herself together and tells Hannah that she could have stopped Helly from killing herself. Hannah told her that she couldn't have done anything about it and that it wasn't anyone's fault. She (Hannah) explained to Nana that it was Helly's decision to make about her ending her life and she told Nana that it didn't anything to do with her. Nana argued with Hannah and told her that she could have stopped Helly or even convinced her not to do it. Nana's face turned white as she slowly walked away from Hannah and Hero. Nana went back up to her room and cried herself to sleep. The next day Nana woke up and couldn't remember anything that had happened the night before.

Chapter 11

The Birthday that will never be forgotten

7th August... Growing up, this date used to bring Hero lots of joy but now, it brings nothing but heartache. It's been three years since Helly died yet to poor Hero it only feels like yesterday. The pain of losing his sister is still fresh, he doesn't like talking about it or her. It's 9:30 am and Hero's still in bed. Last week he told Hannah, his foster mum, that he was willing to celebrate his birthday just a bit seeing as he hasn't celebrated this event for the past three years and he felt like he was finally ready to do so. However, lying in bed on this particular morning, Hero's not sure if he is up to celebrating today. Still lost in thought, Hero turned onto his right arm and noticed a dark blue envelope on his side table.

Hero sits up and carefully unseals the envelope. Inside there is a printed card with HAPPY BIRTHDAY in fancy metallic writing. He curiously opens it and on the inside is a long message written by Hannah. Hero gives a small grin as he reads the words of encouragement and love written by his foster mum. "Maybe today won't be that bad" He muttered to himself. He was unsure if he should take advantage of his special treatment and sleep another hour or if he should get up and face this day head on. He puts the card back onto his side table and goes back to staring at the ceiling.

At roughly 9:50am he starts to get out of bed. Parched, he sits on the edge of the bed and guzzles down a whole bottle of water. After he had a shower, brushed his teeth and changed, Hero's ready to go downstairs but something stops him. From the corner of his eye he caught a glimpse of Helly's suicide note. For years he's been wanting to act upon the note, but has never brought himself to do so. Hero may be physically strong but mentally all the trauma of his past still affects him to this day.

After a few minutes of staring the folded note on his drawer, he snapped his attention back to the hairbrush in his hand. He starts brushing his hair violently, with all his strength, ruining it in the process. Once he stopped, he was panting for breath, his arms ache and his forehead was sweating. He looked at himself in the mirror and he was a mess. As he started to fix his hair properly this time when suddenly he stopped. A flashback of his last birthday with Helly was playing in his mind.

Helly, all dressed up and ready to go to dinner, walks in on Hero who hasn't even started to get ready. "Come on, we're gonna be late", She says while sitting down on his bed next to him.

"Yes, I know. It'll take me two minutes to change. Unlike you" He says with a little smirk.

"What's that supposed to mean?" She playfully demanded while giving Hero a light punch on the arm. "We're twenty now Hero can you believe it?" Helly states, gazing out through the window.

"Eight years." Hero replies. The room falls silent for a minute, an awkward tension enters the room and they can both feel it.

"But we're doing alright now aren't we? We can't change what happened in the past." said Helly optimistic as always. Hero doesn't reply. Helly gets up and starts to leave the room.

"Hero". He looks up at her. "You know I love you right? I always will. No matter what happens to me I want you to remember that I love you. Always be yourself, don't change for anyone!" Leaving Hero slightly confused, she goes back to her room.

Hero's flashback ended and that's when he realised something. Helly wouldn't want him to have to hide a part of himself, Helly would've been proud of him for telling the truth. He decided he was going to be honest. For Helly.

He goes downstairs to the living room and is surprised when his step mother starts singing him happy birthday the second he walks through the door. She hands him a small paper bag which Hero hesitates to accept. Inside the bag is a matt black box. Hero sits down on the sofa and Hannah sits on the sofa opposite. He slowly starts to open it. On the inside there is a shiny, top brand, gold watch. "You didn't have to" He muttered, while taking the watch out of the box and putting it on around his wrist.

"Hero you know I'm really proud of you, your being really brave deciding to celebrate your birthday after everything that has happened." she stated proudly.

"Hannah There's-" Hero started to speak.

"No, I'm not finished yet. I just want to tell you that I love you so much and you're so mature putting on a brave face". You could see how happy Hannah was, with a massive grin on her face, all those years ago she never thought she would manage this but now, looking at Hero, she knows she did a good job raising him.

Hero suddenly started to think he was making a mistake, he had the feeling that maybe Hannah wouldn't accept him being gay. He was about to change his mind, he then thought: Helly would've wanted him to be honest, he should tell her. Right then before he could stop himself he did it.

"I'm gay!"

Suddenly, her smile fell, her face was emotionless. She just stared at the floor, on the inside a storm brewed, she couldn't believe what she was hearing. All of her pride was gone, she felt disappointed, she blamed herself and her horrible parenting skills.

"I'm gay" Hero said more confidently, unsure if Hannah had heard him the first time round. When Hannah heard this and realised he was serious, she was outraged.

Chapter 12

Rage

"What?" She demanded.

"I'm Gay" Hero said with less certainty.

"Are you sure?" Hannah questions

"Umm... yes." Hero was unsure how to answer this question. He doesn't really understand why Hannah is reacting like this. He thought that she would be okay with it.

"Why?" Hannah was asking questions that were difficult to answer.

"This is who I am. Why don't you understand that?" He started to regret his decision to tell her.

"no, no, NO." She was starting to lose her temper. "That is not right! Did I raise you like this? Do you do something like this to your mother?" She exclaimed

"YOUR NOT MY MOTHER!" He shouted at her before he could think about what he was saying.

"EXCUSE ME?" Hannah shrieked. Hero immediately started to regret saying that, he knew that now he will have to face hell.

"I HELP YOU GET THROUGH THIS HUGE LOSS, I TOOK YOU IN, I'M ACTUALLY CELEBRATING YOUR BIRTH-

DAY FOR YOU AND THIS IS HOW YOU REPAY ME?" She continues to shout. "WHY CAN'T YOU JUST BE NORMAL?" This really hurt Hero's feelings. All this time he thought that he could trust her and that she will always love him and that's why he told her first. That's when hero started to think, if she doesn't accept him will society.

"If you could just LISTEN!" Hero pleaded.

"NO, I REFUSE TO LISTEN, WHAT YOU'RE DOING IS NOT RIGHT!" Tears where streaming down her face. Hannah couldn't believe it. What happened to her son? Why was Hero acting like this? This was all she could think of.

"WHOSE INFLUENCING YOU SO MUCH THAT YOU'RE DOING THIS? TELL ME AND I'LL GO SORT THEM OUT!" Hannah was infuriated, she wasn't able to control her temper. She wasn't aware of how much she was hurting Hero's feelings.

"There's no one I'm telling you, please why don't you believe me?" Hero was desperate for her support, she's the only one he has.

"THEN WHO? WHO IS IT?" She was screaming now, nothing could calm her down.

"NO ONE. I MADE THIS DECISION ON MY OWN. I CAN'T HELP THE WAY I FEEL IT'S JUST ME!". He was shouting too. You could hear their argument from two houses down. Without thinking, Hannah slapped him with the back of her hand, right across the cheek. They were both quiet and for a moment time stood still. Hero looked up at her teary eyed. He didn't say anything but his gaze

106

was enough. Hannah's still standing up, adrenaline still pumping around her body. Both were in shock, until Hero broke the silence.

"This won't change who I am" It was a slight whisper but loud enough for her to hear and it was a huge mistake.

This pushes Hannah over the edge. She grabs him by his collar and pulls him up on his feet.

"HOW DARE YOU!" She shouts in his face. Out of pure rage, she pushes him towards the stairs were he lands on his hands and knees. Tears streaming down his face he starts to get back up. Hannah grabs the bunch of keys that have every room on it. She starts storming towards the stairs. Hero sees her and is instantly afraid.

.He starts to sprint up the stairs but

falls halfway through, letting Hannah catch up slightly. She was about to grab him by his leg when he got back onto his feet and continued to run.

"GET AWAY!" He shouted as he was reaching the top. Hero ducked into his bedroom and quickly closed the door behind him. He thought he would feel his foster mum try and force open the door but instead he heard the key being slotted in and the door being locked.

As soon as he realised that he got locked in his bedroom, he started violently banging on the door.

"Hannah, Hannah let me out. Hannah please!" He cried. It was no use, Hannah was not going to open this door and he knew that. Hannah sat on the sofa and cried quietly to herself as she listened to her son bang the door upstairs.

Hero refused to be locked in this house, he started to think of all the different ways he could escape. He could break the door down but then Hannah would realise. Then he saw it, the window. Luckily for Hero, the living room window stuck out in a trapezium shape right under his room window. Without giving it a second thought, Hero grabbed his car keys and opened the window as wide as he could. He sits at the edge of the window and slowly starts to lower himself down. He slips ever so slightly, almost letting out a scream. He manages to put both of his feet on the living room window and stands there for a minute trying to regain his breath. Adrenaline pumping through his body, half of him wants to jump while the other half wants to climb back up to his bedroom. For a moment he actually stood there deciding which one to do. He was just about to climb back up when he remembered the way he was just treated. After recollecting his thoughts, he knew what he had to do. He counted in his head: 3.2.1. He jumped off and landed onto the grass on his hands and knees. Keys still in his hand, he stood up as quietly as he could and made his way to his car.

Chapter 13

The accident

The dark sky roared and lighting struck brightening up the stormy grey cloud that towered over the county as the rain poured down soaking everything. Hero sat motionless in his car overplaying what just happened in his head like a broken movie on repeat but the more he thought about

it the angrier he become and the desire
to escape consumes him. Turning the key,
the engine immediately soared to life, instantly heating Hero as he drove away as
fast as possible; anger and misery still cloud-
ing his mind as he gripped the steering
wheel so tight his knuckles turned white
and his foot firmly pressed against the pedal
making him past the speed limit.

As time went on, Hero's anger fused
and he was grossed in the feeling of hurt
and humiliation. Wallowing in self-pity
salty tears started to cloud his vision dis-
tracting him from the narrow road ahead.
Suddenly, something ran into the road making Hero slam on his brakes hitting his
head on the dashboard in the process. A
loud screech was heard as the rusty old
truck swerves, twists and turns across the

narrow road before hitting the side of the road denting the truck. Hero, taking most of the impact. is immediately knocked out.

Harry drove along the deserted country road looking out his window at the scenery, questioning himself as to why he decides to come out in such bad weather. He suddenly spotted what looks like a massive piece of scrap metal piled up at the side of the road. Coming to a stop it suddenly dawned on Harry that his was not just an old piece of metal but a truck. Hesitantly Harry exists the safe environment of his car immediately getting drenched by freezing rain. He takes long strides toward the damaged truck and used all the strength he could muster to open the door.

Inside was a boy that looked to be around twenty, unconscious. His beautiful face

was covered in purple and black bruises
and his arm was turned inward at a strange
angle as well as his leg. A thick red liquid
oozed from a large gash in his forehead.
Harry is motionless and still for a minute
just taking in the horrifying scene before
him until his mind registers and he frantically calls for an ambulance.

Hero woke to the smell of disinfectant
and detergent invading his nostrils. The
room was silent apart from his heavy breath-
ing and the constant beeping sound to his
left. With a pounding headache Hero sat
up squinting his eyes in an attempt to sharpen
his vision. Looking around he realised he
was placed in a small white hospital room
and questions began to arise in his mind.
He shut his eyes in attempt to remember
what exactly had happened but nothing

came to mind. In fact, the only clear thing he could remember was his name everything else was like a dark fog. The heart monitor sped up the more hysterical Hero became, it was beeping louder and louder which just made him more frantic.

When the white door suddenly opens causing Hero to let out a small screech while looking at the beautiful man that just entered, wondering what he was doing in his hospital room. After what felt like an eternity for Hero the man finally walked up to the bed and broke the intense silence with a warm smile.

" Forgive me if I startled you" he said, "My name is Harry by the way. Harry Smith" Hero remained silent, mesmerized by his charming smile, until finally replying:

"Hero, Hero Thomas." Although it sounded like more of a questions than a statement.

"Well it's a pleasure to meet your hero, although I wish it was under better circumstances "Harry replied flashing his white pearly teeth. Hesitant Hero finally asked the question that had been on his mind since he woke up.

" What happened?" Harry's smile instantly vanished.

" I was hoping you would tell me".

It was later confirmed by the doctor that Hero was suffering from a minor case of amnesia, caused by the large gash to the head, but fortunately his memories would slowly come back in bit and pieces. However, until then he would have to continue staying at the hospital in case of emergency. His foster mum was soon contacted by the hospital and informed of the situation as well as social services who were immediately worried and called a check up on the family.

Meanwhile, Harry and Hero had been chatting happily making each other laugh. Feeling very comfortable around one another bouncing remarks between themselves like a kids ball, their banter was crude and they insulted each other often but no insult was meant to hurt the other. It was simply their way of complimenting one another. Hours later it suddenly dawned on Harry that he has to go, dampening his mood.

Seeing the frown on Harry's face Hero instantly became worried and asked what wrong.

"I'm afraid it's late and I have to leave"

Hero immediately deflates at the thought of being left alone but tries his best to hide his disappointment and gave Harry a weak smile

"That's fine I'm very grateful for everything you've done for me and will forever be in your debt." Harry just gives hero an apologetic smile before making his departure. But not before promising to come back soon.

Chapter 14

Doubt

James' house looked like heaven compared to Rachel's; she'd always thought that a great man would always had an organised home. James' house was so impeccable every time it made Rachel suspicious of him. She shrugged it off like she always does.

"You look beautiful as always" as James kissed Rachel she blushed in embarrassment. Whenever James touched her, fear strolled down her spine which reminded her of her husband. Rachel belly bellowed in hunger. She held her stomach and quickly turned away. James on the other hand laughed like a maniac and asked, "Are you hungry?" Rachel cheeks were flushed pink and she nodded gently. James patted the seat next to him. James laid on the sofa scrolling on his phone and looked for the nearest place to eat. Awkwardly, Rachel stood over him and wondered what to do next. She knew that James got angry easily.

The aroma of spices filled the air and Rachel's stomach growled. As she ate she felt James eyes walk all over her body and face. She grinned. Her grin left her, she felt guilty. James looked at her, confused and worried but then he grinned. Did he like to see her like this?

"James- I need to tell you something."

"What is it?" James asked. Rachel had to tell him before she lost her courage.

"I have a husband. I live with him" she confessed.

"Okay, so?" James was confused.

"Don't you care?" She was confused.

"No, all I know is that I love you and I want to be with you" James pressed his lips on hers fiercely. Rachel felt like something was wrong.

Rachel starts to doubt her affair with James. *I don't know if this affair is worth my relationship with James. I remembered the first time we met, it was so romantic,*

Tom and me were looking each other in the eye and he asked me if I wanted to go to the cinema with him, of course I was in love with him at the time so of course I said yes. It was the first date I had have and when we were in the cinema, he touched my hand and we looked at each other, his gorgeous green eyes stared into mine. She thought. *The second date that we had was a picnic, he told me that he didn't want to be alone and that he had extra food left over. He acted as if he didn't love me but I knew that our one kiss meant more. And I was right it did mean more. At the picnic he asked me to come to his house so we could have more privacy. I loved that day and will never forget it.*

It was so emotional when Tom left for the army. But it was his dream since he was a child, so I let him go. We both feared he would never come back, but he did I missed him so much. He had created a hole in my heart, we called each other every day, but it wasn't the same. She was lost in her thoughts.

Chapter 15

Memories

The stentorian sound of an alarm. Annie woke up as if it's an emergency. She briskly gets ready for work then quietly checks up on her mother, Maria slept peacefully on her bed. Before the day has started, Annie was already in her kitchen, dressed fully and ready to go to work. Before leaving her house Annie grabs her morning coffee and walks outside the door, locking it behind . Annie marched towards her car opened the door gently with her right hand. She drove off leaving the trail of car tracks behind her. You'd think the road would be empty at seven in the morning. Everyone would be asleep, right? Maybe except a few doctors, therapists, and nurses, those important people the world can't live without. It isn't though. Annie's car joined a train of others, mostly office workers with vital' paper to push for twelve hours or more hours.

She finally arrived at her destination, The Letra Surgery. Carefully getting out of her car, she strolls down to the entrance of the surgery, approaching the reception. "Hi, can I have my card to register, please?"

Annie requested to the receptionist. "Sure thing, Annie. Let me just fetch it first." The receptionist replied. As the tall blond hair guy went to fetch the card, Annie found herself being haunted by her past, she pushed that thought away deep inside her mind. The blond hair guy returned with the card. "Here you go." Annie takes the card from the receptionist. "Thank you, Finn."

"Any time." Finn smiles and disappearance into the room once more. Making her way towards her office she wonder what her mum might be doing, is she safe, has Annie made the right decision leaving her alone at the house?

...

On their tiptoes they reached up to the window ledge, eyes wide, hoping to see the first shoots of springs. Just yesterday they planted the bean with their mother. They made little pots using their hands, the black and white strips becomes something new, something that is capable of holding a new life. Oddly, once the soil was inside they became more stale, like proper pots. They stood in a tray, added a beam to each and water too. Their mother told them to be patient, there is nothing yet, but she knew every morning will be the same, standing there on tiptoes until they grow tall enough to be planted in their garden. Falling and tripping over you could hear their sweet, joyful laughter from a mile away, it would echo through the halls and into each and every room in the house, and would cheer the whole entire neighbourhood, it was at times like this that their parents like having reckless kids. The mountain lay in the distance like a ridiculous green camel hump or perhaps the nose of a slumbered giant turned to rock. Two girls explored around the area.

One of them had blond hair which was poker- straight and filled back into a low ponytail. The other one had a tumble of caramel curl fell as she removed her winter toque. As she turned around to her sister her eyes where sky blue and caramel freckles that laid over her nose and upper cheeks ."Annie, Annie" the breathless girl running shouts at her sister.

"Kenya, hurry up!" Annie roars back. Kenya accelerated. "Annie what are we doing? I'm tired." Kenya moans. Annie turns around and waits patiently whilst Kenya catches up, "I told you already, Kenya, we are getting a pretty flower for our flower collections."

"Oh yeah now I remember." Kenya replies flashing Annie a cheeky smile before she chases off into the trees. "It doesn't always have to be a race she knows." Annie shouts back before chasing Kenya down the hills.

...

Once again it knocked the door for the fifth time. Outside the door, the knocker stopped knocking perhaps it was irritated that no one answered. The door creeps open of the office. "Annie! ANNIE! A voice spoke from a mile away. "What?" Annie groaned still deep asleep on her comfortable chair. Realising where she was supposed to be Annie, jerked awake from her wonderful dream.

Chapter 16

Amnesia

Rachel had received a call from the hospital, telling her that Hero was there as he had a car crash. She was already in the hospital as she was having an Asthma check up told by the doctor to remember that Hero had amnesia. She would have to introduce herself again . So she went to his ward. She walks in to the the ward. Rachel tries not to think about incident in her personal life. As she walks in she sees Hero and says hello. She realises that he had no-one with him.

"Is anyone here?" Rachel whispers

"No, who are you?" Hero said in a angry tone

"I am your social worker. I have known you since you were twelve I know you are confused and I will try to help you to answer your questions as much as I can. I have called Hannah, but she is not picking up her phone."

"Who is Hannah?" Hero said confused.

"Hannah is your foster mum, your biological parents died when"

"When I was twelve. I remember." Hero interrupted.

"Yesterday, Hannah called me to say you were gone from home and you had been for a couple of days. All of your things had been moved. We thought you'd moved out without letting her know. Do you remember why?" The social worker explained calmly to Hero

"No, do I have a bad relationship with Hannah?" said Hero, gasping for more air.

"No, but recently I think something has happened between you both and you don't want to talk about it to me. Which I understand, however I do want you two to sort it out soon."

"Oh, okay" Hero said thoughtfully.

"Do I have a foster dad?" Hero questioned.

"No." Rachel replied was finding this hard. The doctor didn't want the fam-

133

ily and friends to give too much information at one time because she didn't want them to confuse Hero. The doctor also suggested that we don't give too traumatic news or words.

She had to keep this in mind. She shouldn't forget this. She was so forgetful these days. It was always Tom that reminded her things like this. Tom. Tom, her loving husband. Why was she doing this to their relationship? What if he finds out about her affair with James? Why was she doing this again? She knew she loved Tom, but was it enough? Does she love James? Does James love her? She knows Tom does. Tom loves her.

"Did the doctor mention when I can leave?" Rachel came back to reality as Hero spoke.

"Not yet, I think you need to take some rest."

"Okay" Hero didn't understand what was happening but he knew he somehow trusted this person.

"I'm going to leave now, is that okay?" Rachel didn't want to leave, but she had somewhere important to be.

"Yeah, I will be fine. You can go." Hero said was sure.

Even though Rachel was worried, she left. As the automatic doors opened she left thinking about her date, with Tom.

Chapter 17

Realisation

Rachel wasn't sure whether she was dreading this date night or whether she was excited. Rachel hasn't had proper time alone with Tom since the start of her affair with James. All she knew was that she had butterflies in her stomach.

Rachel was at the threshold of the front

door. She had had many memories in this house. It

was where she moved after she and her husband got married, it was where she got

pregnant and it was where her son, John, grew up.

Their house was clean but unorganised. She loves her home.

Rachel goes into the living room and sees Tom, he's wearing a white shirt with a black

blazer, his blond hair is pushed back and his gorgeous green eyes stared into

her eyes just like they did the first time they met. He's waiting and smiling

as if he has never seen something so beautiful.

He is attractive and sweet. Rachel feels like this affair is getting to much for her, she has missed spending time with Tom. She walked over to him and then sat down

next him. He moved closer and asked "What's wrong?" He was concerned. Although

it's a good thing sometimes he can be a bit too concerned for Rachel. Rachel

loved this about him. It made her feel like she was loved.

"No, it's okay. I am fine." She tried to convince him.

"No, you're not. Tell me." He knew her too well.

"It's just work. It's okay."

"Tell me"

She had to think quickly. She couldn't tell him the truth. "Well, you know Hero? He has

been in a car crash. He hit his head and

he's got amnesia now."

"Wow, he is such a sweet boy. I remember when he came round here, when you were ill."

"Yeah, I remember." Rachel sighed.

"I made dinner." Tom said, changing the subject.

"Great! What is it?"

"Lasagne, your favourite." He seemed pleased.

"Thank you, " Tom leaned in for a kiss and she let him. He was careful. He made me feel

like he was precious. However, every moment of it was torcher for her, she

couldn't bear telling him the truth, especially when he knew her too well, she

might blurt it out and their marriage would be over.

They walk to the kitchen and sit down. They had a big house every corridor was a maze for

them. Tom had put candles, wine and lasagne. They started eating. The candle

light was making their eyes twinkle. He looked happy, handsome and heart-warming.

It was Tom, Tom was the man I loved. I realized this now. It wasn't James it was Tom. He

did so much for her. He stayed with her through thick and thin. She loved Tom.

"I love you." She confessed to Tom.

"I love you too" And she knew this. However, this was too much for her.

"Excuse me." she went to the toilet to give herself a pep talk.

"By tomorrow you must tell James that it's over, even if you are scared of him, even if you don't

want it to end. Because enough is enough.
You love Tom. Stop wasting your time
with James."

After they finished eating they went back
to the living room and turned the televi-
sion on.

They watch, laugh and talk. The couple end up falling asleep on the sofa, tan-
gled in each

other's arms.

Chapter 18

The Patient

The wind was howling quietly amongst the trees. A small cherry blossom tree arm stretched towards the window making a scratching noise at the window. Three loud knocks were banging on the door once again, perhaps now it was annoyed that no one is saying, come in.' Within a minute

Annie wakes up her face, sleepless. "Come in!" She shouts at the closed door in front of her. Hero walks in, without a word he placed himself in front of Annie. Annie smiles, patiently for Hero to tell her what's going on. "Good afternoon, Hero. How are you today?" He looks at her for a second then looks back at his hands, "I'm fine I guess." He replies feeling shy than usual.

"Is there something I should know about that you're not telling me?" He continues to stare at his hands then slowly he rises his head. "I've been getting flashbacks recently." he hesitates as if he's scared to tell Annie what's going on. "Flashbacks of what? Places, peoples face?" Hero looks up at Annie staring her straight in the eyes. "Flashbacks of a girl and a boy that I think I think that boy might be me. I'm not sure."

"That's a wonderful news, Hero, this means that you're getting your memories back slowly. Perhaps you could draw the girl that you see in your flashbacks, maybe someone might know who she is." Annie smiles and writes about the flashback Hero was getting. Hero spoke once again breaking the silence into a thousand pieces, "I think Harry might be hiding something from me I can just feel it in my guts, you know. It's like he knows something I don't." Annie looks up her smile disappearing into the ocean swore to ever be seen again, instead a concern looks replaced the smile. "Let's talk about the positive chances, shall we?" Hero shrugs his eyebrows lifting up as if to dare her to prove the possibilities of the situation being positive.

"How do you know he's hiding something from you, is it something he does,
something he says or is it his - "Hero cuts
her off, "It's not I don't know how but I
just have this urge feeling that he's hiding
something and he definitely want me to
about it. And if I bring it up he'll try and
change the subject." Hero searches con-
fession in the therapist's eyes but there's
nothing but understanding sparkling in her
sky blue eyes. "Hang on a second." The
therapist replied. As she scribbles what's
been said in her notebook, Hero finds himself in a world of confusion, a brain full of
questions that are about to burst out but
they never explode out they stay there in
the dark.

Annie finally stop scribbling and looked
up. "Harry might not want to makes you

more stressed, perhaps, since you know your accident and all that's been going on lately. You could speak to him confront him, ask him question, show him you care you are concerned, be brave, Harry, this world is far worse than you realise." Annie looks down again scribbling in her note book. A wash of relief is set on Harry's face. "Thank you for your advised I will think about it and make sure I do take some actions positives one." Hero smiles and stands up. "Anything else?" Annie asks. "No, you've helped me enough." He walks towards the door shutting behind him, leaving nothing but quietness that he left behind.

Chapter 19

New friendship

Harry walked through the wide entrance of the hospital and was greeted with the smell of detergent and sad faces. The automatic sliding glass doors closed behind him as people rushed around doing all sorts of things, paramedics wheeling patients on trolleys, one child was in a neck brace another screaming in the corridor as doctors run around. Harry walks towards the reception and gives the name of the patient before he began his journey across the slate grey towards Hero's room. As Harry passes more and more doors his anticipation to see Hero increased, as Hero reminded him of someone he used to know, until he reached a familiar white door with a large plastic sign above it displaying the room number in bold writing.

He pushed open the squeaky door, Harry looked in to see Hero laying in the curtain bed

staring straight up at polystyrene tiled ceiling. Hero heard something and looked to the door and saw Harry, his whole face lit up.

"You came back" he stated.

"Of course I made a promise didn't I?"
Harry simply replied with a cute smile full
of kindness before asking Hero how he
was feeling to which Hero replied much
better. The two boys continued to joke
and laugh with each other until a
painting in the side of the room caught
Harry's eye. In the middle of the blank
canvas there was a perfectly painted girl
with the bluest eyes that showed a beautiful soul and light brown hair that messily
cascaded down her back in waves.

She had a nose like a cartoon character
as if it had been lazily drawn on and
dusty pink lips. Harry instantly recog-
nized the girl and began to get angry.

" What's that?" He asked in a low bitter voice while he glared at the painting,
trying the keep calm. Hero laughed ner-

vously.

"Nothing" Hero started to respond but Harry

cut him off with a roar.

"What the hell is that?" He shouted as he started spilling questions in Hero's direction in a fast pace. Until Hero finally cracked, he stood up and in a low broken voice he manages to whisper,

"I don't know." In a second Harry was in front of him glaring

"What do you mean you don't know?" Harry spat the words out with such hate it made Hero

flinch back and he shrank into the wall.

"I mean I have absolutely no idea who that girl is." Hero sobs in hysterics making Harry

panic. "Ever since I've been here I've

been getting flashbacks and memories and this girl has been in every single one but I have no idea who she is, all I know is she's important!" The words rushed out in a frantic voice that broke half way through as he sobbed the words out.

Harry is still for a moment, frozen, his mind tried to digest what he was hearing. His

eyes desperately searched Hero for any signs of dishonesty and when he came up short. Harry stumbled onto the bed and puts his head in his hands.

"She was my friend.my best friend and now she's gone" Harry exclaimed.

"What?"

Hero started to question but is once again he's cut off by Harry's shout "She was my best friend and she said she would never leave but she's a liar. She left me alone, scared and she's never coming back all because of one stupid, stupid mistake" he bitterly shouted.

Anger, pain, sadness and betrayal was clear in his eyes as he looked at Hero who was

taking small hesitant step towards the bed. "It's okay" Hero said in the softest voice he

could manage as he reached Harry, wanting nothing more than to comfort the boy

that he started to like. Hero reached around and embraces Harry in his arms and

let him cry on his shoulder releasing all the pain and anger he had bottled up

for so many years.

Ten minutes went by in silence neither

boy wanting to move from the others warm embrace.

Both felt safe and peaceful in each other's arms until Harry finally broke away

and wiped his eyes. This left them both cold without the others' comfort.

"I'm sure you must have questions" Harry gently asked, he looked Hero in the eyes as he hesitant spoke,

"You said she was gone...That she left you what did you mean?" Hero inquired in a soft

voice trying not to trigger anything.

"She killed herself" He looked down and answered with a whisper, leaving Hero in a state of

shock where he couldn't help but ask why. When he saw the small tear escape Harry's eye he knew he asked the wrong question.

"I don't know there was. there was no note or letter nothing" Harry replied in a broken

voice as he started to cry again.

After a long silence Hero decided to ask the question that had been swirling around his

mind ever since this conversation began.

"What was her name?" He quizzed, unsure about how Harry would react.

"Helly." Harry mumbled. Instantly Hero was shaking.

That name. Where have I heard that name? He asked himself. Just then

memories started playing in his head. Him and Helly on his birthday. His

parents. Their funeral. Helly dying.

Coming out. Hannah's abuse. Escaping
through the window. The car crash.
Nana's nursing home. Finding the letter.
The
letter. Overwhelmed by all these memories, tears started streaming down Hero's
face.

Chapter 20

Trouble for James

Hero suddenly shoots up from the chair. "I know where he is." Hero exclaimed in a low but vexed voice. His head was fuming.

Harry walks down the stuffy hospital corridor looking at the bizarre paintings on the wall until he reaches an all too familiar white door and gently pushes it opens it to see Hero sitting on his bed frantically putting his shoes on. His dark hair furled down the gape of his neck while his fringe covered the right side of his face, going a little past his jawline. "Where are you going?" His eyes were bold, darker than usual and his voice was firm but so soft too it made Hero surprised. "Harry?" Hero breathed looking at him with disbelief in his eyes "What are you doing here?" Hero says nervously. "Thought I would visit and now I'm glad I did. Tell me where you are going?" his voice unwavering and direct. Hero sighed "James's house."

"As in - James Smith!" This makes Hero snap his head up to Harry "You know him."

Hero said voice bitter while stared expectantly at Harry "Yeah...uh he dated Helly." Harry hesitantly replied and scratched the back of his head he avoided eye contact with Hero. This just made Hero more annoyed "You didn't think to tell me."

"I didn't think it was important." Harry glared in Hero's direction but his answer seemed to push Hero over the edge, "It wasn't important?" Hero laughs sarcastically. "It isn't important that my sister had an abusive boyfriend that drove her to kill herself!" Harry stared into Hero's bright blue eyes that burned with anger, "Answer me!" Hero screamed but Harry's lips where paralyzed in fear. "If you knew about him about the abuse why didn't you help You could have helped but you did nothing and now she's dead She's dead and

161

it's all your fault!" Hero's words fall out of his mouth in rage. The words hit like a bullet in Harry's heart "I didn't know. "like a broken down radio he repeats again and again torturing himself, "I have absolutely no idea...about you about the abuse... she didn't tell me anything."

Hero snaps "Some best friend you were she had a whole secret life ahead and you didn't even know about it? ...you never cared about her that much" Harry as he glared at Hero like he wanted to kill him with his eyes at that very moment, "How dare you! Of course I cared about her. Hell, I loved her." Harry retailed making Hero sneer at him as the heated argument continued with a war of words both trying to hurt each other until the other backed down.

162

Harry yelled "Where were you when she was alone and in trouble, don't be a hypocrite." Hero's eyes widened and scowled at Harry, who was standing at the door and said in a low voice full of determination "I might have done nothing then but that about to change." Hero stormed out the door leaving Harry confused, concerned but most of all hurt.

Chapter 21

The Confrontation

Hero looks up into the clouded sky for the last time; he starts the engine. Hero speeds down the road like this was his last chance - his only way to avenge his sister. A new rage has lit inside of him - or was it

always there? The buildings where a blur;
just like Hero's mind. His memories where
back but why did it feel like a part of him
was still missing?

His wheel's scream. The acceleration
high. Hero's mind aggrieved. Only a road
lay between Hero and this man. What had
he done to Hero to make him pained? The
car came to a holt. Hero had arrived. He
slammed the car door shut. Picked up the
huge, rugged stones. Like a catapult, he
started throwing the stones towards the
house, he didn't care which direction and
were the rocks were going but the house
that looked a shed before now looked even
worse. The owner came out. Blood drip-
ping down his nose.

"Hero?" asked the mysterious man.

"James" Hero felt revolted when he said

those words. "You killed her. Your murderer. HOW DARE YOU LIVE!?" James, who is distressed about his fight with Rachel, had eyes like a hungry lion about to pounce on its prey. Hero started to cower. "Little boy, even if I did push your sister, who by the way was the one chose me over you, why come here? Aren't you afraid of being killed by me? Wait, aren't you the only one left in your family, Hero?" James laughs, even though the blood continues to drip.

"Don't you dare talk about my family like that! You are just a coward, who bullies others so you can get rid of your hatred. But let me tell you something, that feeling of loneliness you have, will never disappear, it will follow you everywhere you go, like your shadow and you can never get rid of it - do you know why?" A cold, hard silence filled the space.

"I don't need to know why." James exclaims casually.

"You do. The least you can do is carry the guilt of her death...I will make sure every day of your life is a living nightmare. I will make sure to wipe that idiotic grin of yours." Hero wide eyed and ready to take down his prey.

"I'm making you annoyed- that is a good start. But can we talk about why you destroyed my house again? Dude, I'm a murderer, not a thief, I can't afford to repair this." James joked and laughed. From a distance, anyone could see Hero's veins bulging from his forehead. "Are you a physio or pure imbecile, who likes to abusive people to death? How can you just joke around while someone died because of you? Unless you've... abused other women before?" Hero glares at him from afar; the tension is strong enough to cut with a knife. "First you accuse me of your sister's death then you make the random assumption that I have abused her and other women. Are you sure that you don't feel guilty for not noticing that your sister was, you know, a bit crazy. I noticed it too, she seemed to be not normal...like she was - what's the word- mental. Just like you."

A punch broke out; releasing all the nestled feelings of fury inside Hero's heart. One blow after another like a synchronized routine bruising James' chiselled jaw. How dare he! How dare he, laugh and live while my Helly is dead. A blow to James' chest. Hero's sorrow and hatred was enough to drown a city in flames. To Hero's surprise, James doesn't fight back he takes it all. James face was bloody. He eyes blackened. His symmetrical face is unnoticeable in all the blood. James looked up. His eyes full of wrath. Slap. Hero was down with one attack. "Get out of my face kid. Leave, before I kill you like I made your sister do to herself."

Slam. The enormous, oak door shut, thankful the only thing that isn't damaged in James' house.

Hero, on the floor, severely injured after one hit. He looked up towards the sky and the clouds started to disperse and the blue sky could be seen once again. His thoughts turned into a stream of calm water. "Helly, my sweet little sister, I am so sorry. Why didn't I realize what you were going through? You came home every day and acted like nothing was wrong. Every time I asked you if you were okay, I should have known something was wrong, something was behind that innocent smile of yours. So-rry Helly...H-elly"

Footsteps. The sound of gravel was getting louder and louder penetrating Hero's eardrums.

Hero's eyesight a blur, the hit was worse than he thought. "Hero!" The voice seemed so familiar like Hero knew this man. "Harry?" Painfully and excruciatingly slowly, Hero started to get up from the floor, Harry helped him up. "What happened? Did you fight? With him." Harry pointed towards James' front door in surprise. Hero nodded uncomfortably. "Why are you here? I thought you were angry with me?"

"I knew you would come here and you would get hurt so I had to know you where ok. I had to know that you weren't hurt. But you clearly are, like I knew you would be."

"Why? Why did you have to know?"

"You have no one else that knows that you are here. Only me. So let me take care of you. Please."

Hero stumbles to his feet. Harry scowled towards James' house. His eyes were full of resentment and loathing. "Harry, don't." Hero leaned against Harry's broad shoulders. Harry snapped back his attention to Hero, who was still in immenseness pain. "I can't believe he dared to hit you after knowing what he had done to Helly." Harry caressed Hero's injures gently, like he was touching glass. "Hero...let's go home."

174

Chapter 22

Everything's Back To Normal

The winter time had passed in its sombre majesty: having brought Annie skies of richly marbled greys and trees so elegant in their bare beauty. Those cold days for calmness and reflection are waning and a new energy rises. On this spring day, Annie sees the flower that are to colour Annie's world for the warmer days to come, waving in the breeze like a smile born of the cosmos - happiness in brilliant shades. Annie lets her eyes flow from tree to tree, noticing the buds ready to open into the light, to be as green flags in ever-warming wind.

After a couples of months Annie's mother is out of the hospital, she is very pain and weak. Helplessly, Maria apologizes for everything she's done and the burden she's put Annie into. Maria spoke her lips trembling, "Darling, I'm really sorry for all the burden I've put you through." Maria started to cry a clear crystal tear making its way down her rosy pink lips. Annie walks towards her mother and gives her a long light hug, "It's okay, mum. Please don't cry. I should be the one apologising to you for not handling the situation well. What's important is that your alive nothing in the world means more to me than that."

The mother's love Maria has for her child is ordinary kind, she just regrets the fact that she didn't handle her husband and daughter death well. It is more than any mother Annie knows and respect. It is the kind of love that would move heaven and the Earth for her child if she has the power. It is the kind of love that say, "I would give you my life for my child any time, any place." That doesn't make her unusual, after all she was only normal. Maria just desperately wishes to change back time to not make the foolish mistakes she made with her beautiful daughter, Annie.

The spring days where spend in the garden, Maria and Annie. They planted their runner beans, courgettes and more. There where the days of bright sunshine, blue skies that sung of the summer to come: there where the days of cloud- filtered rays, the ones that made the world so cosy. There where the days it began to rain, and instead of dashing inside they stayed in the garden talking, dancing laughing, to taste that feast of water. That was there world, the two, happy with the Earth, sunshine and rain.

Maria couldn't mourn the copper statue in her yard losing its shine, it can no more resist that can. But then in recent years it has begun to oxidize and I find the green-blue bewitching, enchanting. So now with each passing year it becomes more beautiful; She can hope that is what she does too. Not physically of course, let's face it, it's mostly downhill from twenty and the slope only gets steeper from forty. No, she hopes to become kinder, wiser, more true to the person her inner child always asked her to be. Perhaps as the wrinkles deepen over her face so will the positive effect of her life on others. She wants to slide into middle age with grace, not with an almighty splurging tantrum. But for now she will just sit with her tea and watch the birds, the statue and the joyful growing of the spring plants in the yard.

Chapter 23

The Demand

In the hospital the doctor tells Annie that her mum is okay, however the payment has had an increase. As Annie has just finished her work she, is on her away to the hospital to see how her mum is doing. The hallway has as much personality as the rest of the hospital. The floor is slate grey and the walls dove. Above the ceiling is made from those polystyrene square laid on a grid like frame. The light is too bright for Annie's eyes after the darkening gloom outside. Above every door she passes is a large plastic sign, dark with white lettering - no fancy fonts, just bold and all-caps. It's so new and spotless Annie feels like the whole building must have just gotten beamed here from some-place dirt is outlawed. Her eyes fall to the garish flowers in her hand, their dampness seeping through her woolly glove. Suddenly Annie don't mind the flowers' cost anymore, it's worth it, Maria is going to need some colour in this place. As Annie is walking to see her mum she is thinking if for mum is ok and if she wakes up from all the drugs she has had. As she was outside of the mum room the doctor called her name "Annie come over there", Annie was nervous because she thinks that her mum has taken more drugs again. The doctor said "have got the bills for you mum". Annie replies back to him, "Okay." As Annie takes the bill her eyes are wide with fear and frustration. "How can the cost be this much!! Do you think I was born yesterday to not realise that you are blackmailing me?" Annie depends to the doctor. "Look the situation of your mother is no joke her operation is very serious and we are doing the best we can to provide her with such care." With a sigh Annie apology to the doctor and goes to visit her mum whilst thinking about several ways of owning the money.

As Hannah just got up to make herself

a cup of tea, there was a sudden knock
on the door. When Hannah opened the
door, Annie the therapist, came running
into Hannah house to talk to her about
if Hannah can give Annie a paid because
Annie can't pay the all of my bills. Annie
"Hannah I need that money today or you
can just pay me more" Annie said angrily.
Hannah replies with "I can't pay you more
I need this money for myself". Annie said
to Hannah "you always help me; come on I
need this money" Hannah replies with "Ok
I will give you more money this is only".

Crystal like tears make a small river
down her face. They were indeed the tears
of joy. "I don't know how to thank you.
This means so much to me. Thank you so
much, Hannah, thank you." Annie's voice
breaks into a sob. Hannah carefully ap-

proaches her and pulls Annie into a hug. "Your mum's going to be okay, lovely, everything is going to be okay." Her soft voice clam her a bit. Annie wished that was true she wished she had some kind of hope inside her but now even the thought of hope angered her it seemed like just a word with no meaning. Nowadays, Annie just thinks that someone drawn a black curtain around her. She knew her days will be forever dark and gloomy but she still she had to try even if it meant to become a whole different person. Annie couldn't lose her mum not a chance she's the only one Annie has and without her there wouldn't be a world without a mum for Annie.

Chapter 24

Realisation

Rachel was at the threshold of James house. She was worried, scared, angry. Why did he not tell her about how he abused Helly. She went inside before she changed her mind. James was there waiting for her, in the living room. She stared at him, standing, waiting and wanting him to tell her about him and Helly. She didn't know how he would react. He then patted the bit of the sofa next to him, indicating to sit next to her. She was standing still.

"What is wrong?" James had asked.

"Nothing, I have something to tell you..."

"What happened?"

"I'm ending this relationship." James stood up, trying to control his anger.

"Why what happened? Did your husband find out?"

"No I made this decision myself. I don't want to do this to Tom. I love him. You were just a phase."

"I WAS JUST A PHASE!? ARE YOU LISTENING TO YOURSELF?!! YOU LOVE ME! IF I TELL YOU THAT YOU LOVE ME THEN YOU LOVE ME!" He slapped her and then grabbed her wrists and twisted her arm so she couldn't move. She screamed in pain.

"Tell me you love me!" He spat it at her in her ear.

"HELP!! HELP!! HELP!!" Rachel screamed hoping that someone next door would hear her. James slapped her mouth so she couldn't talk. She then bit his palm. James yelled in pain and stumbled back. Rachel ran for it and broke into the car and started the engine. Then she drove like mad, to her house. Then when she was in her driveway she stopped to breath and gathered her thoughts. She then got her phone aher nd called the police and told them everything that happened. She decided she would tell husband about her affair and not about how he hit her.

A few minutes later. She went inside

her house. Sitting there was her husband. She couldn't wait, she had to tell him and face the consequences.

"Baby?"

"Yes?"

"I cheated on you. I'm really sorry. You can hate me all you want but please don't leave me" Rachel started to cry

"Please" Tom came over and hugged her.

"It is okay." Rachel could hear him she was too busy crying.

"Babe. Stop. Look at me." Rachel looked up into the eyes she fell in love with.

"I'm sorry"

"I know and it is okay."

"What?!" Rachel was confused. She thought he would leave her.

" I need to tell you something too. I

kissed one of my colleagues."

Rachel thought she would be angry but she was actually glad. She wiped her tears.

"Lets both forget this and move on. We are probably going to laugh over this in the future."

They both laughed. They loved each other. They then made up with a passionate kiss.

Chapter 25

94 Days In Prison

James stared into the cold, icy life that was now his. *Prison*. Fear and a sense of unwelcoming lingered in the air. The stench of sweat and blood filled his nose. Four solid, white walls stare back at James;

a metal bed stood in the dark corner of the room; a bucket isolated on the other side of the room; and a small, barred window with a whimpering light only barely lighting it. James sat on the grim bed and stared at a paint drip.

Walking down the inhospitable corridors. Everywhere he goes he sees a reminder of his dad.

"What are you looking at." The prisoner took his hand out from the bars and grabbed James neck tight

"I need you back up on perimeter 116." The guard outside the bars says through this walkie talkie, when he sees James being staggered.

"You think that you're such a tuff boy, don't you, but on the inside you know that you're not and your scared that you will

die alone." The stranger prisoner continues.

"Hey let go!" James cries. The prisoner
lets go leaving a purple mark on James
neck.

"You wait until lunch, pretty boy". From
the insides James was burning. He wasn't
ready to face someone as tough as that yet.
He needed to toughen up.

That lunchtime he beat up the man and
his gang,

That'll teach them not to mess with
me' James thought to himself, although
this didn't help him with his prison sentence being extended, it did help him get
rid of some enemies. Every single day, for
ninety-two days, he didn't make any new
friends, although it may seem like a bad
thing, James got used to it. On the ninety

third day the prison guards made an arrangement to see a therapist.

A Women gilded towards James's cell. She had that shy look young women often have, but it was never morose. Behind those slightly pursed lips were a smile just waiting to be tempted out. The woman outside the bars wouldn't have looked out of place with an office suit, yet she was dressed in a casually tailored suit and her hair was salon- perfect. She spoke,

"Hello James, the prison guards said that they are worried for you and they thought that it is best for you to start seeing me, I'm a therapist. I know it may seem hard for you losing your mum and your..."

"I don't care about them; they were useless anyway." His hands were holding tightly on the bar, as if at any moment he could break though and crush her.

"I don't need a therapist i'm doing perfectly fine." James snapped.

"Well that's not what the prison guards think...look if you think you need help from me about your anger issues, all you have to do is ask the prison guards." She left silently as if she was never there in the first place.

By the next day James was talking with the therapist about how embarrassing he felt for yesterday and how today he is trying to make a fresh clean start. "I'm sorry, yesterday wasn't a good day for me. It was the day my mum died from cancer in the hospital."

"Oh I'm sorry for your loss, believe me from experience I know how hard this can feel"

"You never told me what your name was."

"Oh, I'm sorry I was called in such a rush yesterday that I forgot to mention my name. I'm Annie. Now James tell me why you got in here?"

"It's because that Rachel girl, not only betrayed me but she also dumped me."

"You need to realize that what you did was wrong, if you want to get away from here."

"How about you tell me why you feel angry."

"I... if I tell you then you must promise me never to tell anyone about this conversation."

"What do you think I'm here for, whatever you tell me would stay in this room.

Mark my word for it." Annie replied answering patiently for James to speak.

"Okay. My anger all started when my mum...died" he paused for a second as if he only realized now that his mum was dead. "When she died everything changed, my dad was different. He said that I must go to school by myself and that he won't take me home from school. He quit his job and we had to live off benefits, it was so difficult and a huge change in my life. One night I remember him telling me to come down, he had beer in his hand, it must have been empty because when he threw it at the floor all that came out was glass, he used to make me run around and lift up my top only for me to get cuts on the back several times." He took off his top and showed her the scars on his back. They were all knife cuts "That day...that day I will never forget."

Annie's face was drawn white with shock. "Oh my goodness. It must have been tragic having your own father abuse you like that."

"It was the first few times, but I got used to it."

"I know this must still be hard for you but you need to learn to forgive and forget, although it may seem hard to forgive him in order for you to continue with your life you need to." He looked down at the floor. "Can I visit their graves?" James asks.

"If it will help you in your progress." Annie replies with a kind smile.

The next day James was allowed out of prison to see his father's and mother's grave. "Can I have some time alone with them?" James asks.

"Of course." Annie walked off.

"No matter what I say I will never forgive you for what you did, and although seeing me going to jail may make me pathetic but I will never forget what you did to me. I will take my revenge. Believe me, I won't die alone and i will keep fighting for my freedom. I want you just to remember what happened when you were at the hospital that day." James turned around as if what he said really changed him as a person.

"Have you forgiven your father?" Annie shouts from the distance eyes sparking.

"Yep, and I feel so much better, I really think that telling my dad how I feel is a good start to recovery."

Chapter 26

Revenge

James looked at his tiny window, a breeze of fresh air hit him. He couldn't see anything outside. "Alright everyone go to sleep, James, you have a busy day tomorrow." The prison guard explained in excitement.

"How come?"

"Because today was your last day in

jail, didn't you count the days."

His face lit up, today was the last day that he was stuck here.

"No." He closed his eyes.

"James, James, your hurting me, please let go! I love you but you always do this and Hero is starting to realize my bruises."

"I can't let go." However no matter what he says she keeps on repeating.

"James please let go!" He sees a bright light and everything changes. There is a girl, she has brown hair. James gets a closer look. Her eyes are brown. "I've seen you before."

"James, James why did you do this to me." he turns her around, only to see a skull "Why did you do this to me." Suddenly James is sinking into the floor, everything is different now. This room is familiar to him. "James come down here right now." James go downstairs, there is a man with beer in his hands. "Dad."

"Why to do it, why did you have to kill my wife." He breaks the bottle and picks up a piece. "Turn around!"

"I'm sorry, I was a young-"

"Turn around!" Out of the corner of his eye he can see a Shadow, it's a man.

"Hero?"

"You killed my sister, she gave you everything."

"I'm sorry I didn't mean to."

"It's too late and it's all your fault."

He wakes up, no one's there. James is covered in sweat and out of breath. He looks around the room "Helly" but there's no one to hear him. Although it takes a while he manages to go to sleep.

He collects his valuables his car was in the parking lot, he went into his car and got home. At his house he has re-decorated everything, now the gloomy walls have been coloured to a nice bright cream, he has a new sofa and all the chairs have gone in the bin for new ones to come. Although he didn't like it he needed something to fool the therapist. It took him four months to update his whole house. On the left hand side of the room is a bookshelf. James walked up to the bookshelf and moves it to the right hand side of him. There is a hole in the wall. It looks like a passage-way. James is very proud of what he has built and thinks that it looks very hidden, he walks through and closes the door be-hind him. There is a staircase, it's like a hidden basement. At the very bottom there is a cork board with two faces and a rubber band, James has OCD and it has to be perfect otherwise he breaks it and throws it in the bin. He has been spying since they met.

"Don't worry I've made sure that you will get what is coming. Three years have passed since Helly, although she wasn't my intentional victim she still got what was coming to here, however now my list has grown soon Hero and Harry will be no more. I've always hated love and wanted to destroy it, same with you Rachel you may have Tom by your side but prison has made me stronger than ever and anyone that tries to get in my way will die, " his face had a big grin. He went back upstairs and was about to watch TV until there was a knock on the door. "Okay remember James, you have to be positive and happy."

"Hello?"

"Oh, hello come inside."

"So how have you been doing since you got out of jail." It took James a long time to answer

"I've been doing great, as you can see I have given my room a new look."

"That's good, so you don't feel angry anymore."

"Yes."

"And you still feel okay about your father." On the inside he would have broken her neck and hidden her in what he calls his secret lair.

"...Yes" Annie stood up and shook his hand.

"I'll be back next week to check on you

again"

He closed the door and went down stairs. "My father destroyed my life, although that is bad enleast I now know the potential that I can do. You wait for what I have coming up dad, just because your dead doesn't mean you can't suffer. And you Hero, thinking you could take me on, your because not only did I beast you up but I also realised that you have a weakness, Harry. Rachel ooh I have something even better for you, I will kill your husband and make you suffer before killing you. Everyone will suffer just like me, knowing how it feels to be broken.Two at his father's grave the bricks had been broken and there was still paint drying, this paint said this is only the start' "It's just like they say revenge is a dish best served cold"

Chapter 27

Forgiveness

Hero sat rigid on the marble counter-top in Harry's bathroom as Harry gently cleaned his wound, there was an uneasy tension in the atmosphere as an awkward silence settled between them, both wanting to talk but either quite knowing what to say as they stole secret glances but desperately trying to avoid eye contact. Hero grasped his sweaty hands together and hisses as Harry dripped alcohol in Hero's injuries

"I'm sorry". Hero finally let out before he could stop himself

"I didn't mean anything I said I was just angry and took it out on you which wasn't fair at all and I'm so, so sorry"

Hero apologised which made Harry smile softly

"It's ok we were both angry and said some things we didn't mean. I'm sorry to." Harry said

just as softly before going back to treat the wounds. As Hero takes the time to

admire Harry, his smooth pale skin, his thick eyebrows that curved in concentration, his dark and luscious hair that made Hero want to run his fingers through It and finally his chocolate brown eyes that held so much emotion it made Hero's heart hurt.

"Why are you looking at me like that". His rich silky voice broke Hero and threw his daze, without thinking he responded.

"Because I love you." This made Harry freeze and that was the only word that came to mind.

"What?" he said in a whisper which made Hero panic as he nervously started to justify
himself.

"I mean you have been there for me since the start and you make me feel safe and happy which I haven't felt since my sister died and I want to be with you but I understand if you don't feel the same I mean you might not even like guys... Oh

God I'm so stupid sorry I'm so sorry I

don't want to ruin this friendship just forget I said anything." Harry cut off Hero's rant when they pressed their lips together in a passionate kiss.

They pulled apart and took shaky shallow breaths connecting their foreheads as Harry

whispered softly:

"I love you too" Before pulling Hero in for another kiss.

A week later, Hero got a phone call from a much too familiar number. Reluctantly, he

picked up the phone.

"Hello?" he answered.

"Hero?"

Hannah's croaky voice spoke through the phone. Hero could instantly tell that she'd been crying. For some reason he felt guilty.

"Hannah." Hero replied, trying not to act friendly.

"I need to speak to you." Hannah requested.

"If you think I'm going to go back to that house and live with you again then you're

mistaken." Hero told her sternly. Tears started spilling down Hannah's face. The

call was silent for a minute.

"Please, you don't have to come home, I could meet you somewhere, the park?" Her voice

sounded brittle. Hero could almost feel her anguish through the phone.

"Ok fine, I'll meet you in half an hour." Hero told her and hung up the phone before she

could argue.

Just like he said, half an hour later,
Hero met Hannah in the park where they
both found a bench and sat down. At
first it was awkward, they were both avoid-
ing eye contact, neither one of them knew
what to say. It was a nice summer day,
there were children running around, and
families having picnics. The happiness around
them largely contrasted with the tension
between the two. Eventually Hero decided
he wanted to break the silence but wasn't
sure how. Hannah was preparing herself,
she felt like any minute now, Hero would
lash out at her and tell her what a horrible person she's been. In her opinion she
deserved it.

"So go on." Hero encouraged.

"What?" she asked, momentarily confused.

"You said you wanted to talk to me. So talk." Hero continued.

"Oh Hero, I'm so, so sorry, " she sobbed, "I don't know what came over me, I just got so

angry." Hero wasn't sure what to do or how to react. "You know I went to church every single day and I prayed and prayed for forgiveness about the way I treated you." Tears were now spilling out of her eyes and Hero reached to her face and wiped away her tears but he still didn't say anything.

As Hero's moving his hand away from her, she grabs it and holds it gently between her own. Hero thinks about pulling away but he doesn't, his love for his foster mum is too strong despite what she did to

217

him. "You know I was worried sick about you, especially when Rachel told me what happened." She continued to sob

"If you were so worried, then why didn't you visit me?" Hero inquired.

"I couldn't bring myself to, I was the reason you left the house in the first place." Once

she confessed this she started to feel even more guilty than before.

In a way Hero understood this, she was the reason he lost his memory but Hero was grateful. If that didn't happen then he would never have met Harry or faced James, something finally felt right to him. He had closure. A few moments went by while both of them found the courage to speak. "Hero listen, you have to believe me when I say that I'm really, truly sorry about what I did. It was cruel and unfair and unjust and." she fell silent. She knew saying all of this won't make a difference, she did what she did.

"Why aren't you saying anything?" she begged Hero. Hero was unsure about what he was supposed to say. A football started rolling towards them and Hero kicked it away. He kept his gaze on the floor, he was really unsure how to react, he thought Hannah would never forgive him. "Hero." He looks up at her, tears starting to form in his eyes. "Please, come home." She pleads.

Hero did not respond, instead all he did was cry. Big fat tears ran down his face like a waterfall but no sound came out of his mouth. Hannah sat there for a few minutes thinking Hero was furious that she made such a request but when she dared to look up she saw a painful sight. Seeing Hero's silent cry fractured her heart into a million small pieces. Without hesitation she started uncontrollably sobbing. When Hero saw Hannah crying he embraced her into a tight hug despite what she did. The mother and son stayed like that for a long time and got many weird looks from people passing by but they didn't notice.

After a while, when they had both calmed down, Hannah sat back and looked at Hero straight in the eye. "I don't mind." She told him.

"Sorry?" Hero didn't understand what she was talking about.

"You being gay." she confessed. "I thought about it, a lot, and if that's really who you are then I don't mind." Hero couldn't believe what he was hearing.

"Really?" A small smile started to spread across Hero's face as he realised she was serious. She nodded "Yes, really!". They hugged each other lovingly, they had each other again and they were happy. Afterwards they both strolled home together. They didn't say anything but there was nothing that needed to be said.

Hero gets home and started to paint, and thought about everything that has happened recently and how the events of the past helped him build up the strength he needed to deal with these situations. He sat down and thought about the future and how things have changed, as the paint started to dry. *THE END*

Our Authors

Hannah Conlon

I would like to thank my family for always being there for me and my friends are always there. I would like to thank myself for getting through this stressful week, also my best friend Cleo Gaynor my little chicken nugget for always being there when I need her help. I LOVE my Netflix and McDonalds. I love playing football it's my life.

Cleo Gaynor

This has been stressful week but I have finally got through it with my best friend Hannah Conlon who I have helped a lot. I love doing cheerleading, it's one of my favourite things to do in life, it's who I am. I love eating McDonalds with my friends and family. I love spending time with my little sister, she means the world to me.

Harinie Suthakaran

This has been the most stressful and tiring week of my life and I thought we would never get a book published but we did. I would like to thank everyone who helped write this book. Also, thank you to my parents for being supportive this week. Also, I can't believe that you actually bought this book, thank you. I can't believe we are all published authors!

Maria Qayyum

I'm 14-year-old who has a big dream of becoming a doctor. I have a brother his name is Sikandar Qayyum. I have a sister called Maira Qayyum. I have loving parents, Hina Qayyum and Abdul Qayyum, who always support me through thick and thin. Firstly, I'll like to thank my family and friends for always being there for me when I needed them the most. I'll like to thank my parents for giving me permission to contribute to writing this book. Also I would like to thank my school for giving me this huge opportunity. Finally, I would like to thank my friends Hannah Jacobs and Esme Oliver for their support.

I had such a great week missing my subjects but stressful because I need to catch up on those subjects, and communicating and working with others. Lastly thank you for Eleanor Dixon and Joe Reddington for their time and effort for helping us out.

Mahnoor Khan

I would like to thank my school for giving me this amazing opportunity and before this week I never thought that me of all people would ever become a published author so this is certainly an achievement. I would like to thank my family and my friends Pavleen Kaurana, Reshicca Ragu, Sabika Ahsan and Elina Chaudhary for supporting me throughout this process. And finally I would like to thank Eleanor Dixon and Joe Reddington for all their guidance and help with this project.

Isabella Smith

I would like to thank my mum for giving birth to me, my nan for supporting me and my school for giving me this amazing opportunity, along with my teacher Ms Durcan and the rest of 9A. I would also like to thank Isabella Fisher and Isabella Ilhan for having such an amazing name, Shawn Mendes for being the love of my life, my six horrible siblings, Rossana B for showing me what real music is and Ruby S, Millie Clay and Fatima Mahamid because they asked to be mentioned and finally I would like to thank myself for just being all round amazing.

P.S Future Isabella when you are reading this laughing at yourself remember how stressful this week has been.

Schana Ghafury

I am thankful for all the support we have had from Eleanor Dixon and Joe Reddington for helping us through this stressful week of writing the book.I honestly didn't think we could finish it because at the beginning we had 65 chapters to do but we managed to get it to 28. I would also like to thank my parents and my family for helping me get through this tough and stressful week and for everything they have done for me there are no words that could describe how thankful I am to have such a caring family. However much I do won't be enough to repay them but I would like to get into medicine and pass my GCSEs to make them proud. My hobby is hairstyling and I love watching Netflix and having fun with my family and friends. Anyway if you are reading this I want to say thank you for buying this book and reading it also there may be some mistakes since we had so much to do in one week.

Kira Lim

I would like to thank my family for giving me the support to do this and my teachers for helping me catch up with all my work and picking me to do this. Although this wasn't easy we managed to come up with a book under five days and I am very happy for that. I would like to thank my friend Harinie for helping me come up with James ideas and sorting out the timeline. My mum and my nan have both been very supportive and nice to me, letting me have such an exciting opportunity. I would like to thank my mum for surviving me telling her the same plott over and over again. And I would like to thank you for buying this book and taking your time to read this book. Thank you.

Ridwaanah Alamin

I would like to thank my family and friends for supporting me. I would also like to take this opportunity to thank my mum and dad for all they do for me (even if I don't tell them that, that much). Also Harinie, who made us organized. I am proud of all of us for writing, proofreading, editing and publishing this book in 25 hours.

Printed in Great Britain
by Amazon

34097271R00138